MW01230105

STAY WITH ME

The Vigilante Hitman, Book 2

KELLY MOORE

Edited by
CALEB MAU
Illustrated by
BEST PAGE FOWARD

Kelly Moore

For Diana Macquen,

If anyone deserves this book, it's you! Thanks for being so dedicated!

PROLOGUE

John

a burning pain smolders in my chest, and when I strain my eyelids open there is nothing to see but infinite blackness. Not a single speck of light trickles through the dark. I have no idea where I am. The last thing I remember is being on the boat with Miles, my brother, and Brooklyn.

Brooklyn.

Is she okay? Where is she? Where am *I*?

I try to sit up, but the pain in my chest is blinding. It hits me full force when I use my hands to try and push myself up. I scream out in agony, clutching my shoulder as I curl into a ball on the hard, damp floor. The scent of mold and mildew is strong enough to taste. As I wither in pain, the dirt and grit on the floor grind into my naked flesh.

A chill runs through me and I realize I am wearing nothing but a wet pair of boxers. Where are my clothes? How long have I been out?

I close my eyes to the darkness and listen carefully. The sound of water dripping into a puddle echoes to my ears over a mechanical hum in the background. Intermittently breaking up the somber rhythm is the sound of footsteps. The sharp tapping sounds like an expensive pair of dress shoes stepping across a dirty cement floor, and the footsteps are coming quickly toward me.

Before I can pull myself together to prepare for whoever or whatever is coming, I hear metal grinding against metal as a latch is unlocked and a heavy door is opened. Illuminating beams flood in, temporarily blinding me. My eyes must have been closed for a while, they're so sensitive to even the smallest amount of light.

I cover my eyes with my hand as I try to peek through the gaps in my fingers. All I can distinguish is a dark silhouette with a bright, white glow shining behind it.

"Well, well, well. I was beginning to wonder if you'd ever wake up." It's Miles. I can tell from his short, round outline, and his annoying voice: like nails on a chalkboard.

"Where am I? What did you do to me?" My throat is sore and gravelly. I didn't notice how thirsty I was before, but now that I try to speak, my body is screaming for water. Hell, I'm so thirsty, I'd drink battery acid if offered to me.

He walks toward me into the center of the room, where he reaches up and pulls a chain. The light flickers on and I squint against it. "I told you what would happen, didn't I?" He holds his hands out at his sides.

I force myself to look at him as I sit up right. "Where is she? What have you done to her?"

He laughs a deep belly laugh as he slides his fat little hands into his suit pockets and begins pacing back and forth. His dress shoes slap hard against the floor. "Now, John. You don't think I'd actually hurt her, do you?"

I shift my weight to try and stand but fall back down. My head is spinning and my vision is doubling. What has he done to me? I feel like I've been on a week-long bender. My stomach rolls and my mouth waters, preparing to empty my stomach.

"I wouldn't move too fast if I were you. You've been through quite a traumatic experience." He's wearing a crooked smile and his dark eyes gleam with pride.

"Where the fuck am I?" I scream. My voice bounces off the concrete walls and floor and echoes back to my own ears.

"You're back in Chicago." He smiles. "Back at the club, actually. Don't you recognize it?" He motions with his hands around the room even though there is nothing that indicates I'm at the club. From the cinderblock walls to the dirty concrete floor, I can't tell anything other than that I'm in a basement of some kind.

I lean back against the wall, still sitting on the dirty floor. I pull my knees to my chest and rest my elbows on them while rubbing my throbbing head. "What did you do to me? I feel like I've been drugged." Even my words sound slurred.

"Many times. I had to transport you somehow. And with your gunshot wound, you should be happy you've been sedated."

"My gunshot wound?" I'm confused for a moment, but the sudden realization brings the pain slamming back to my chest with full force.

Memories flood my thoughts: being on the boat, Brooklyn being held at gun point, getting shot.

"You son of a bitch," I growl while looking up to his pompous face.

He holds up his hands innocently. "You really gave me no choice, John. If you would've done your job, none of this would've happened. You and your brother would both be free men."

I jerk my head back up. "Where is he? Where is Brooklyn?"

His pacing starts back up. "They're fine and they will continue to be... as long as you're a good boy." He walks in front of me and stoops down to my eye level. "You're mine. You owe me for all the trouble you caused. Do you even know how much business you cost me? People think that I can't control my men, and we can't have that." He grabs a handful of my hair and jerks my head to the side to force me to look at him. "Can we?"

He's fucking lucky I'm so fucked up or that would have been his last move.

"Can we?" he roars in my face with a sharp jerk on my hair.

I have to swallow my pride and bite my tongue for now. "No," I answer flatly.

He releases me. "That's what I thought." He stands and walks back to the center of the room before turning to face me again. "You're going back to work, John." He smiles before turning off the light and leaving me alone in the dark. It doesn't take long for the shadows to swallow me up again.

CHAPTER ONE

John

My fingers have traced the photo so much over the last few weeks that the image is already fading and the corners are curling inward. I slam my hand against the cold metal wall, listening to the same echoes that I have been listening to for... how long now? It feels like forever. My hand throbs from the impact.

"When are you going to let me the fuck out of here?" I yell. My voice travels down the corridor and vanishes into empty space. I sit on the damp, uneven concrete floor, hanging my head between my knees. My sense of time is gone and I have no idea where I am. My captors have drug me from place to place with a bag over my head so that I never know how far I've traveled or where I am. I have stuck to my guns and refused every one of their demands, but they've finally pulled out all the stops. This goddamn photo they brought me is my breaking point.

I trail the tip of my finger across the picture, tracing her long, deep red curls. God, what I would give to run my hands through the silkiness of her hair, to sweep it out of her face as her dark eyes take me in. The little boy is the spitting image of me, there is no denying that he is mine. Everything about him looks like me, down to the color of his hair. Those eyes though, they are Brooklyn's. He has that same spark in them, like hers. The way she is looking at him, I know he saved her from being all alone. I can tell she has poured every ounce of love she had for me into our son. He didn't even exist for me until Miles shoved the picture in my face. The bastard taunts me by telling me that I don't exist for them either. I'm dead. I'm a dead man locked in a cell, in God knows where. All I have is a tattered pair of jeans, an old t-shirt, and this picture.

My hand voluntarily finds the star-shaped scar on my chest. It's raised and still tender to the touch, shooting flares of pain whenever I exert myself. I overheard Miles telling one of his men that the bullet is still inside me. He mumbled something about *'nanotechnology at its finest'*. The short little fucker had it all planned out. He never really had any intention of killing me, at least not physically. He drugged me that day on his yacht with something that stopped my heart long enough for Brooklyn to think I was dead. I could hear her screaming my name, but I couldn't move a muscle or utter a word to tell her that I was still alive. The specially-made bullet went in and cauterized the vessels to keep me from bleeding out.

Even if I could escape, the titanium bracelet snapped around my wrist would leave me even worse off than I am now, and likely endanger my family. It is as much my captor as Miles is, with sensors that will alert my guards if I get within a hundred yards of the perimeter. According to Miles, if I try to escape I will end up a pile of ashes from a powerful jolt of electricity that will travel straight to my heart, stopping it in an instant if I'm not back on the property within minutes of triggering the alarm. The memory of his belly shaking with laughter at the thought of incinerating me makes me sick to my stomach.

I don't know why he's kept me alive. Killing me would have been easier. He says he has plans for me and until I agree to work for him again, this will be my punishment for not killing the woman that I love and costing him millions of dollars. His fucking greed has changed him from the man I once knew, someone I considered a friend.

The sound of boots pounding down the hallway rouses me to my feet. I take three steps back, knowing the door will open soon. The rattling of the keys always puts me on edge, filling my head with thoughts of a freedom that has yet to come.

I glance at the worn-out photo one more time and shove it in my pants pocket. I'm determined this time will be different. "I will find a way back to you, baby," I whisper.

"John, you ready for your nightly interrogation?" the stocky guard I've come to know as Tank says with his usual ugly, deep scowl. His bulky biceps protrude from his tight uniform as he flexes his arm with a Taser outstretched, fingers toying with the trigger. The bastard enjoys causing me agony. He's tasered me many times for his own entertainment.

"It's what I live for." The sarcasm rolls easily off my

tongue. Besides, I know it pisses him off. I guess that makes me as sick as they are, finding pleasure in their anger, but the pain they cause me is the only thing that is real to me anymore. His hand clutches my tattered t-shirt and yanks me out the door, shoving me against the concrete wall. I hold back the groan of pain that tries to escape.

My bare feet slap the floor as I straighten my spine and walk beside him. I lost the privilege of wearing shoes when I tied my boot string around Tank's neck. I suppose that's why he feels the need to carry the Taser, other than the fact that he enjoys it. His rough, large hands were around my throat when Miles ordered him not to kill me. I could feel the last breath leaving my body just as he jerked away from me. I wanted to die so Miles would lose.

The windows lining the hall are securely boarded up, banishing all light from entering. The only light comes from the florescent bulbs hanging from the ceiling. Every other one either flickers weakly and intermittently to life or is altogether dead. I've been held here long enough now that I know exactly how many lights there are and how many steel beams line the ceiling from my prison to the interrogation room.

The sound of the keys clanging against the colossal belt supporting Tank's protruding gut grinds on my nerves, but also gives me an idea. I slow my pace so that he is only one step ahead of me, then reach over and rip the keys off his belt, the leather breaking from the force. Before he has time to react, I jam them into his carotid artery. His hand flies up to his neck as the thick, crimson blood pours out of the gash and between his fingers. It's running down my arm, but I refuse to move until he is lifeless on the ground. His knees slowly start to give and a gurgle erupts from his mouth. I move with him to the floor, watching the light fade from his repulsive green eyes.

I look around to make sure no one is coming and quickly remove his boots, putting them on before taking off at a sprint in the opposite direction. The door at the end of the hall is locked, so I take a few steps back and run, ramming my shoulder into it. The hinges shudder and loosen from the impact enough that my second run springs the door wide open.

Sunlight glares in through an open window, momentarily blinding me. It's bright but the cool air bites at my skin. I finally regain my focus and rush to the window. When I look down the three stories, my heart hammers in my chest. I could make the jump - I've trained for shit like this - but I've been locked away for so long, I'm not sure I can make it without breaking something. I look around for other options, but nothing presents itself. The stairwell leading down is blocked by a massive, locked steel gate.

I hear boots barreling in my direction. I have no other choice. The window refuses to budge open, so I take off my shirt, wrap it around my balled-up fist, and punch through the glass. Shards rip at my skin as I climb onto the ledge. The wind whips around me, making me shudder. The only warmth I feel is the heat of my own blood dripping from my fingertips. I look down, hesitating only for a moment, then jump. I tumble through the air and land on my hand against the icy ground. It buckles underneath me, bones audibly snapping and shooting a blast of pain all the way up my right arm. The pain is some of the worst I have experienced, but there is no time now to think about it. I roll over and see two guards looking out the window that I jumped from. Both of them raise their guns and take aim at me. I dive to the left as quickly as possible, just as one of the bullets whizzes past my shoulder. I don't wait for them to fire off another shot.

The ice crunches underneath my boots and the cold air is so bitter on my bare skin that it takes my breath away. I round a corner out of sight and lean against a wall while holding my arm to my chest. I'm on a loading dock. The light on my bracelet begins to flash red instead of the continuous green. *Shit. I don't have much time.*

Movement catches my eye. There is a man on a forklift heading my way. I drop low to the ground and wait for him. He doesn't see me coming until the last minute. He tries to swerve, but I'm able to jump in the seat and grab him in a headlock. The forklift jolts us forward as he slams on the brake.

"All I want is your cell phone."

He responds in Russian. Great, the one language I don't know. I can barely move my right hand, but I manage to pull off the phone that is clipped to his work belt. I know this is my one and only chance. I let go of him as he passes out and jump to the ground. The guards are already coming around the corner, I can hear their shouts echoing down the dark alley. I quickly text a message for my brother to the last number I remember, hoping like hell he still has his burner phone. If he gets it, he will know without a doubt that I'm alive. As soon as I'm done, I throw it on the ground and smash it under my boot.

I stand tall waiting for the inevitable. My body hits the ground hard again as three of them tackle me. I don't fight them. I've learned I will only lose. I will pay a dear price for trying to escape, but this time it was worth it. I know Jake will understand my message. A broad fist covered in thick rings comes flying toward my face. I feel the crack of pain. Before my eyes go dim, I look for any signs that might tell me where I am.

———

"WHY DO YOU ALWAYS DEFY ME, JOHN?" I HEAR HIS voice and feel the slap to my already sore face. "Wake up!" he yells.

My eyes flutter open. Miles is standing in front of me on the opposite side of a steel table. His hands are splayed out, supporting his weight as he leans over, glaring at me. I scan my surroundings. I'm tied to a chair, back in the familiar interrogation room. "Don't you ever grow tired of this game?" Blood flies from my mouth when I speak, sprinkling the table between us. His eyes flash down to the blood splatter and a wicked smile tugs at his lips.

"When are you going to learn that I will win? Now you've gone and killed Tank. I'm afraid you've really pissed off some very dangerous people." His head leans in the direction of the one-way mirror.

I don't know who is behind it, but I know they have been watching me all this time. "Why don't your cowardly friends come out?" I yell.

Miles scrapes a metal chair towards him across the dirty cement. He sits directly in front of me and pulls a picture out of his shirt pocket. "I have a new picture for you. You've been long forgotten, my friend." He places it on the table directly in my line of vision, holding it in place with his grubby fingers.

"Brooklyn has taken up with your brother Jake, and he's raising your son." He laughs. It's a picture of Brooklyn, Jake, and... *God*, I don't even know my own son's name. They're sitting on a blanket spread out on grass. Jake has his arm wrapped around Brooklyn's shoulder. She looks so happy with him. I squeeze my eyes shut to keep them from tearing up. Miles jerks my head up by my hair. "I want you to look at what you've given up your life for. She's moved on."

My entire arm is throbbing, but what I wouldn't give to knock the teeth out of his round, little head. His chair rocks back when he stands. He walks behind me and wrenches back my broken hand, filling my world with agony. The sudden blinding pain pulls an animal scream from deep within me.

"All you have to do is agree to join our team again. I have a really big contract, and you're the only agent that could pull it off. I've been waiting all this time, but I'm losing my fucking patience with you." The warmth from his breath is on my ear, causing my blood to boil. "You have left me no choice." He walks back in front of me, yanking my head back up to look in his beady eyes. "If you don't take this contract, I will kill all three of them."

"If you lay one fucking hand on any of them, I swear to God I'll cut your fucking balls off and feed them to you one by one." Sweat, the byproduct of my all-encompassing anger, explodes from my pores.

He steps back and laughs, the sound echoing off the bare walls. "Not only will I kill them, but I'll kill the boy first while his mother watches."

My jaw flexes in anger and my nostrils flare from trying to keep my emotions in check. I know all he wants is to get me pissed. I won't give him the satisfaction of seeing it.

He takes a few steps closer and leans over me. "Can you imagine? She had to watch you die, only to relive all that anguish by watching the only thing you left her be taken away by the same man."

"We don't kill innocents! We never have!" I yell, losing the raging battle within me.

"If you would have killed Brooklyn instead of playing hero, we wouldn't be in this mess. You forget, when you took down the pharmaceutical companies, you made a lot of enemies. You are only alive because of me." He points at his rounded chest.

I pull at my restraints. "You call this living!"

"It's your choice, John. What's it going to be? You have about ten seconds to decide before I put a hit out on your whole family."

I stare at the picture. I can't let them die. "I'll do it you slimy little bastard. Just leave them the fuck alone!"

"Untie him," he tells one of the guards, "and see to it his hand gets set. He will start his training tomorrow."

As my binds come loose, I rub my swollen hand and watch as Miles leaves the room. I gained two things today. One: hopefully I got a message to Jake. And two: I know that I'm still in Chicago. As soon as I get the hell out of here, I know where to get my hands on some weapons. They have made the mistake of keeping me on my turf, and I will take full advantage of it when the time is right.

CHAPTER TWO

Brooklyn

"I got the lighter fluid!" I yell while opening the screen door.

"We're in the kitchen" I hear Jake call out. When I walk in, he's opening and shutting drawers and J-Man is sitting in his booster seat at the table.

"What are you boys doing?" I set the bags on the counter, pulling out a box of cookies I bought for John. Let's be honest though, they're actually for me. I'm lucky I was able to get my figure back after John was born with my appetite.

"Crayons. J-Man wanted to color. I found the coloring books, but not the crayons." He walks over and takes the cookie from my hand as I'm raising it to take a bite. He quickly shoves it into his mouth.

"Hey, those are not for you!" I swat at him as he dodges away.

"I'm trying to save you from having to lose a few pounds." His finger points at my hips.

"I'll have you know I weigh less than before I was pregnant." I punch him in the arm. "Unlike *you*. You've gained a few pounds the last couple of years." I smile, knowing it's because he's finally healthy. John squeals and says, "cookie," while motioning with his little hands. I take two out, hand him one and put an entire cookie in my mouth before Jake can steal it. He just laughs at me.

"So, where do you hide those crayons?" He sits beside John.

I walk over to the china cabinet and open the middle drawer, causing a phone to slide forward into view. "Is this yours?" I hold it up and turn toward Jake.

His smile turns to a frown. "Yeah, I forgot I put it there." He walks over and takes it from my hand. "It's the burner phone I bought when we were on the run with John." He flips it over in his hand, inspecting it like just seeing it again brings him closer to John.

"Why do you still have it? And better yet, why is it at my house?"

"I carried it around with me for a while, thinking John may call me on it. It was the last phone I spoke to him on and I couldn't force myself to get rid of it. You came in one day from playing with J-Man outside and it had been in my hand. I didn't want you to see it. I forgot that I had stashed it in here. I'm sorry, I'll get rid of it." He starts walking back over to John, pressing the power button on the phone as he takes his seat.

"You don't have to get rid of it because of me. I understand why you would want to keep it. I used to check my phone every night to see if he had left me a message." I walk over and place the crayons down in front of John. He grabs them and starts scribbling in the coloring book.

Jake stands and scoots his chair under the table. He walks over to the wall of cabinets and picks up my phone charger that's plugged in next to the coffee pot. He plugs the phone in and sets it on the counter before grabbing the lighter fluid. "I'll go start the grill." He walks toward the door, but before he steps through, he pauses and looks back at me. "It's a little ironic that you found that phone on the two-year anniversary of his death," he says before walking out and closing the door behind him.

While John colors, I pull out the hamburger meat and start forming it into patties. I'm lost in my own thoughts, reminiscing about the time I shared with the only man I've ever loved. We never really had a time together that was peaceful; yet somehow in all the madness, we fell deeply and passionately in love. I sometimes wonder what his reaction would have been when I found out I was pregnant. I know I was in complete shock when that little blue line appeared. The first person I wanted to tell was John. I even picked up my phone to call him before I remembered he was gone. An hour later, after the tears subsided, my shaky hands were finally able to call my dad.

As soon as I whimpered into the phone, I heard him dismiss whoever was in his office. "What's happened, Brooky?" His voice was quiet, waiting for me to give him more bad news.

"I'm pregnant," I cried out, and he cried with me over the phone. Not because he was unhappy about me having a baby, but because he knew how much I missed John. He knew I could raise a baby on my own, but he also knew how badly I didn't want to. It still breaks my heart knowing that John never met his beautiful son. He looks so much like his father that sometimes I have to smile to keep from crying when I look at him. Not that Jake doesn't look just like him too, but the two of them are so different, they don't really look the same to me.

I'm thankful for Jake being in our lives and loving J-Man like he was his. He helped me pick up the pieces after John died. He cried when I told him I was pregnant, but they were tears of joy. He was glad that a piece of John would live on through a child. He was my Lamaze coach and he insisted on being in the room when he was born. He's been here ever since. He's my best friend and I feel completely safe with him around, but I've never once had the feelings for him like I did with John. They are two completely different men and my heart still belongs to John. Jake and I talked at length after the baby was born. I didn't want him to feel obligated to stay with us. I wanted him to have the life he never got to when he was sick. I wanted him to find a woman and fall in love, having a family of his own someday.

I remember him saying, "You and J-Man are my family. I made a promise to John to take care of you if anything ever happened and that's what I plan on doing for the rest of my life. I can do that and still meet a woman someday."

And he has. He bought the place right down the road from me and opened a garage where he spends most of his time. He even built a rather large pole barn on his property once the business took off and outgrew the small garage attached to his house. Who knew he was so good with his hands? Working from home, he's always around any time I need him to watch Little Man, and he comes over practically every day for dinner. We've remained so close that he's no longer only John's brother – now he is my brother as well.

He has dated a few women since we moved to Hawaii, but he never seems to keep them around very long and sometimes I think it's because of me and J-Man.

His voice jars me from my pondering. "The grill is ready, how about those burgers?" The screen door slams behind him.

I quickly pound out the last patty and wash my hands. "All done," I say, handing him the platter. "Let me grab the cheese for you." I open the fridge and throw cheddar cheese slices on the plate next to the burgers. "Why don't J-Man and I come out and swing while you're cooking?" I ruffle his mop of hair before I pick him up.

"That's a great idea because I think it's supposed to rain later." He opens the screen door and I head out to the swing set. Jake puts the burgers on the grill and I put J-Man in his toddler swing, fastening him tightly in the seat. He giggles as soon as he starts to move.

I watch the sway of the swing in a trance, back and forth, back and forth. My mind slips again to John. Not a day goes by that I don't think about him. He used to occupy my mind in every moment of every day, but time has healed some of the pain. Now when I think about him, I smile. My thoughts go to his touch that I still crave so much. I grin, thinking about how much he loved being in control and how well he controlled my body. I had no restraint when it came to him. I would let him fuck me anywhere and any way that he wanted. He used to tease me about my crown slipping because I wasn't prim and proper. I love that he brought out the side of me that was willing to submit to whatever he wanted. I would frequently turn the tables and gain control over him, which I secretly think he rather enjoyed. I can still recall the sounds he would make when my lips were wrapped around his cock. The taste of him no longer lingers, but I can still close my eyes and see the pleasure bound on his gorgeous face. I miss his touch, his kiss, his breath at my ear, claiming me as his.

After he died, I got as far away from politics as I possibly could. I didn't want anything to do with Washington DC. I slipped out of the limelight and never looked back. After excitement of a cure for cancer faded into the background, my name finally quit being big news. I have a small research lab here on the island. I still seek cures for diseases, but all my findings are registered under a false name, with no links back to me. My latest research involves the cure for Alzheimer's, but I've only just begun to scratch the surface with my findings. Who knows?

Maybe in my lifetime, I'll find the cure for that too. Except this time, I won't be naïve about it. I won't bring danger to my son. I don't need the money after the millions I earned from developing a vaccine against cancer, but I love the research. It helps keep my mind off losing John.

"You okay?" Jake's voice startles me. He didn't make a peep as he walked up beside me.

I blink back the tears that are forming. "Yeah, I'm alright." I smile, but I know damn well it doesn't light up my face. J-Man's head bobs to one side in his swing. He's fallen sound asleep.

"Where were you? You were lost in John again, weren't you?" His hand reaches out and stops the swing.

"I guess I was. Nothing new," I say, unlatching the swing.

"I miss him too, you know." He picks up John and cradles his head to his body. "I'll go lay him down."

I take a deep breath to chase away my thoughts and reign in the dark emotions lurking in the shadows near the forefront of my mind, greedily trying to free themselves. Sometimes I swear I still feel him near me and I get goosebumps. I've been promising myself for weeks now that on the two-year anniversary of his death I would finally let go. I'll truly start over. His memory will never die thanks to his son, but I will force myself not to get lost in him anymore. My life starts over today. I clinch my jaw in determination and wipe away the last tear that I will allow to fall. "I love you, John," I whisper, "but it's time to finally let you go."

The smoke flowing out of the grill draws my attention away. I pick up the bottle hanging from the side and open the lid to douse out the flames. Apparently the burgers are done. I place the slice of cheese on them before I take them off.

Back in the kitchen, I place the burgers on the buns and fix Jake a plate with all his favorites. There is potato salad made with no pickles (Jake hates pickles), baked beans, and his favorite flavor of Doritos – Cool Ranch.

He walks back into the kitchen with his eyes fixed on the burner phone charging on the counter. He picks it up, unplugging it, and sits down. I slide his plate in front of him and he finally looks up at me, blinking back retained tears. "I'm going to get rid of it," he says, as he turns it on. I smile and pat his hand.

I make my own plate and sit beside him. He sets the phone on the table next to him. As he picks up his burger to take a bite, the phone dings with a message. We both stare at it in shock for a moment. "It has to be an old message," he says, turning his gaze toward me.

"Are you going to open it?" I ask, almost in a whisper.

He slowly reaches for it, suddenly jerking his hand back as if it's on fire. He looks at me and I nod at him for encouragement. The scene plays out before my eyes in slow motion as he picks up the phone and scrolls down to open the new message. The soft ding as the message appears on the screen seems to fill the entire house with sound. His mouth hangs open and he's wide eyed staring at the words.

"What does it say?" My voice trembles in anticipation of his answer, whatever it may be.

"It says... *Stand By Me*." I hear the breath he was holding escape as he reads it.

CHAPTER THREE

John

*B*efore the guard can reach for me, I grab the picture off the table and slip it into my pocket. I'm jerked out of my seat and led down the long concrete hallway. There are two guards this time, and each has a hand on one of my biceps, making sure they have me under control this time.

Instead of them leading me back to my prison, I'm pushed into a small bathroom. The floor is the same dirty concrete as the hallway and my cell, but the walls are made up of a dingy, white tile. The mold growing on the grout forms thin black lines between the filthy squares.

A drain sits in the floor directly below a shower head hanging from the open pipes that line the ceiling. A toilet and an old, green sink are against the other wall. The mirror hanging above it isn't glass - it's stainless steel that has been screwed directly to the wall. This place really is like a prison.

A bottle of some kind of universal shampoo and body wash is shoved against my chest. "Clean up, and then we'll take you to see the doctor to have that hand of yours fixed." He turns to guard the door. "I sure do hope you heal fast. I can't imagine the kick-back of a gun with a broken hand."

I scoff and turn my back to him to remove my boots and jeans. When I'm completely bare, I step under the shower head and turn on the water, letting it rain down on me.

It takes several minutes before the water warms up but it feels heavenly. I don't even know how long it's been since I've last showered, but the hot water streaming over my sore body makes me feel like a real person again.

"Time's up, pretty boy. You're not getting ready for a date," the guard says.

I turn and look over my shoulder at him before shaking my head and turning off the water. He hands me a towel and I dry off while looking at my blurry reflection.

Being held captive for so long has caused a lot of muscle degeneration, and my skin now clings tightly to my bones. The scar on my cheek is nearly covered by the overgrown scruff on my face. My entire body is marred with marks of torture. My chest is littered with small cuts and circular burns from my many years of torment, each carrying a distinct memory of pain and anger that have lingered long since the wounds have healed. The circle-shaped scar on my chest, just below my left shoulder, I still recall the smell of burning flesh as it was scorched beneath Miles' cigar.

After I dry off, a fresh pair of clothes is shoved toward me. I pull on the jeans, T-shirt, socks, and boots, and stand up straight. "Can I at least get a razor?" I ask, rubbing my jaw.

He lets out a small laugh but sticks his head out of the door and says something to the other guard.

A few minutes later, a disposable razor and shaving cream are handed to me. I lather up my face and drag the razor across my skin. My beard is long and thick from not shaving in so long, and the hairs stick between the blades. I have to rinse it and tap it on the edge of the sink to clean it out before swiping again.

I splash water on my face and pat it dry, looking closer at the man in the mirror. I don't even recognize him. His eyes look dull and hollow, like he has nothing left to live for. Dark circles line them with small wrinkles at the edges. I look like I've aged a decade in the time I've been here.

The puckered scar on my cheek is jagged and ugly, and my hair is longer than I ever let it grow.

Brooklyn probably wouldn't even know me if she ran into me on the street. Hell, with my deflated muscles and scarred up body, she'd probably run for cover.

I hand over the used razor and shaving cream and ask for scissors, doubting that he would give me a sharp object. He probably fears that I would stab him with it.

He lets out a long breath and shakes his head before handing the items back to the guard outside the door. "The haircut will have to wait, pretty boy. Dinner is served and then we have to get that hand looked at." He grabs ahold of my bicep again and leads me back into the hallway where the another guard takes ahold of my other arm.

I'm led up a set of steps where we pause to let the guard open a heavy, metal door. When it opens, sunlight steams through and I blink back tears brought on by the sudden brightness.

I'm pushed through the doorway and into a big open room. The floor is covered in a dirty gray carpet, and the walls are plain white, but this area is at least clean. This must be where the guards stay while they're keeping an eye on me.

Part of the room is sectioned off, being used as a kitchen. There is a small table in the center, with a fridge, stove, a few cabinets, and a sink.

I turn and note the other side of the room. The wall furthest away from me is covered in brown paper, like it is lined with windows that overlook the hall.

I continue to take the place in, trying to figure out where I am. There is a couch and TV, and further away is a bed. This room almost looks like it was once used as some kind of office. There are several desks pushed to one corner of the room and one directly in the center of the floor, covered in computer monitors. Looking closer, I see my cell on one of them. There is also a camera in the hallway outside of my cell, one in the interrogation room, and one on the entrance of the building.

I strain my eyes to see what is printed on the glass door of the building. It says, "Smith and Stocker Pharmaceuticals".

I don't have a chance to process my thoughts before I'm shoved into the chair at the table.

A plate is set in front of me and I look down at it. A steak – grilled to perfection – steams tantalizingly in the middle, surrounded with a baked potato and some steamed vegetables. "If you're going back to work, you need your strength," the guard says as he sits with me to eat.

I shrug. "I won't complain. Anything is better than the cans of beans and Spam that have been thrown at me."

He stands and grabs two beers from the fridge and hands me one. I'm almost taken back. I stall before taking it.

He urges me on. "Makes you wish you would've given it up years ago, huh?"

"Years?" I look over at him. "How long have I been down there?"

"Down there?" he asks around a mouthful of steak. "About six months. But you've been held captive for over two years now." He cuts a big chunk of steak off and shoves it into his mouth, chewing loudly. I push the anger down and cut into my own steak before taking a bite. My mouth waters from the delicious taste. It's been too long since I've had real food.

There is a long silence while we both sit eating. Then I finally ask, "Why are we in a pharmaceutical building?"

His blue eyes flash to me. "Your girlfriend shut it down with her cure to cancer. The place couldn't stay afloat."

That makes me smile, an action that feels foreign to me. I'm glad her cure was finally released and is saving people.

With that thought, I pull the picture out of my pocket and look at the three of them. My brother is healthy and in this picture, he looks happy.

Happy with *my* family.

What if he loves her? What if she loves him? For two years now she's thought that I was dead. What if she's moved on? Will she even want me back when this is all said and done?

Anger floods my body again, and more than anything, I just want to kill the guards and run from this place. I contemplate it for a moment, staring at the steak knife curled in my fist. I want to find my family and forget all about these last two years. I can't put them in danger though. I will do as Miles demands. I will do this job and be done with it all. I know the chances of getting my family back are slim to none, but I have to end this. I loosen the death grip I've had on the knife.

I want my family back. I want my life back. And I want Miles dead, once and for all.

He says my family will be safe as long as I do what he says. But he's forgotten one thing: I can't be trusted.

I've already fucked him over once, and I'll do it again. I will make him pay for the pain he's caused me and my family.

If it's the last thing I do, I will kill Miles and get my family back.

I'm taking Brooklyn back.

She's mine and always has been. Even before I knew it, she belonged with me.

When dinner is over, I'm pushed over to the couch to wait for a doctor to come in and set my hand. Within twenty minutes, he walks through the brown-paper-covered door and I see that I was right - from the small peek I got out the door, it is definitely a hallway.

He walks over to me and sets his bag down. "This is going to hurt like a son of a bitch," he says as he grabs my hand.

I hear a loud pop and everything goes black.

————

I WAKE SOMETIME LATER SURROUNDED BY DARKNESS again. I'm back in my cell – I recognize the damp feeling and the overwhelming smell of mold. I stand from the cot and walk to the center of the room to pull the chain for the light. A soft glow fills the room and I look down at my bandaged hand, gently flexing my fingers to test them out. Pain shoots through my arm, but I groan and shake it off.

After all this time, I've gotten weak. But it's time to get back to work and I need to be strong.

I sit down on the dirty floor and start a round of sit ups. The real food fills me with energy, but my heavy stomach feels different than what I'm used to. It's almost weighing me down.

I push through it and do a set of thirty sit ups. I'm sore and covered in sweat by the time I finish. My stomach rolls from all the activity and I rush to the toilet to empty its contents. I rinse my mouth out with the sink on the back of the toilet and spit it out into the drain. I pace the room, feeling the anxiety raise inside of me.

I'm ready to get out of here. I need out of here. I want this shit done.

I throw myself down on the cot and place my one good hand behind my head. As my eyes drift closed, I'm flooded with memories: Brooklyn's smile, the way her dark eyes would light up, her soft, cream-colored skin, the way she would feel so tight and hot when I entered her, the sounds of her heavy breathing that would fill up the room when we made love. It's the only thing that has gotten me through this.

Memories of our short time together. It's all I have left to live for now.

CHAPTER FOUR

John

I hear the metal lock being unlocked and then the heavy door is opened, scraping on the floor. I open my eyes to see the hallway light spilling into the darkened room. Before I can sit up, one guard is grabbing me and another one is pulling a black bag over my head. I don't fight them this time, I just let them take me. This is the first time I haven't been drugged for a move.

"Time to go to training, Pretty Boy," the guard says as they lead me across the floor.

"Aren't you guys forgetting something?" I joke.

"Not this time. The boss man wants you alert, not fucked up."

They direct me up the same stairs that I walked up yesterday. Since I memorized the layout of the room, I know exactly where I am. I listen closely and I hear them opening the glass door that is covered in the brown paper. I can distinguish the sound of the paper scraping the edge of the floor as it's pulled open before I'm pushed through it.

Now it's time to pay attention. They guide me to the left and I count my steps. It's exactly twenty-four steps until I'm turned to the right, then another fifteen when I'm turned to my right again. We stop and I make out the ding of an elevator, followed by the sound of the big door sliding open. I take the few steps in, feeling the presence of the men on each side of me. I detect a button being pushed, and the doors close. The elevator begins its slow descent.

I count again. It takes thirty-six seconds before I feel the elevator stop and the doors open. I'm led through what I assume is the lobby, and then I feel the sun warming my skin. I'm outside. The wind blows through my thin T-shirt, slicing through me like a sharp blade. Despite the biting cold, it feels refreshing. Other than my short escape the other day, it's been two years since I felt the heat of the sun or the wind caressing my skin.

What I wouldn't give to be on my bike again, to feel the adrenaline pumping through my veins as I fly down a long road, darting between cars. Just thinking about it makes my heart pound.

One of the guards places his hand on my head and shoves me down. I half expect to hit the hard, icy ground, but instead fall into a cool leather seat.

Within a few minutes, the two guards are inside the car with me and the engine starts up. The radio blares a song I've never heard before, and chilly air blows through the open vents. I shudder from the frigidness hitting my bare arms and I lean back, crossing them over my chest to try and stay warm.

I'm not cuffed or tied down in any way. Why would I be? If I even try to make a run for it, my family will be their target. But that only reminds me of the bracelet that is around my wrist. "Hey, what about this bracelet? Shouldn't you take it off?" Fear suddenly takes over.

"It has been reprogramed for the time being. You're allowed off the property, but it can be turned on at any time so don't get any bright ideas."

I hear him shift the car into drive and my thoughts stop while I pay attention to the direction he's driving. I begin counting. I close my eyes and feel a left hand turn that causes my body to lean to the right. I count again.

I keep all this stored in the back of my memory. On the off chance that I *do* find myself escaping, I'll know right where to go to find Miles.

The car stops and I feel the winter air rush through the interior as a door is opened. Moments later, my door opens too and I am pulled from the vehicle. The wind bites at my skin again, but we must be out in the open now because they are damn near forcing me to run.

I breathe in deeply, but smell nothing but ice and... *Is that gasoline?* I think to myself as the familiar smell burns my nostrils.

I can feel the moment I'm inside. The warmth of the sun is gone and the cold breeze has stopped, but the building is still freezing, as if it isn't used frequently or kept heated.

I'm walked through the building until one of them place a hand on my shoulder, stopping me. After a quick knock, I hear, "Come in." It's Miles. His voice is muffled behind the closed door but it already sounds like nails on a chalkboard to me.

The door is opened and we walk inside. I am shoved into a chair before the guards jerk the bag from my head. My eyes land on Miles on the other side of the desk.

He smiles a welcoming smile. "John! How you doing now that you've come out of the dungeon?" He fills the room with his deep belly laugh.

I tilt my head to the side and pop my neck with no sign of emotion on my face. I get comfortable in the chair, crossing my ankle over my knee. "Well, I'm here. Now what?"

His smile falls just a bit but he quickly recovers. "It's time to start your training. Let's see if that hawk eye of yours is still a lethal shot."

I raise my eyebrow in surprise. "You're really going to give me a loaded gun right now? Aren't you afraid that I will just kill you all and be done with this bullshit?"

He stands, adjusting his expensive jacket and straightening his crimson-red tie. I can only imagine the blood that is all over his hands is the same color. "You don't think I haven't thought of that?" He takes a few steps to the side of the desk and sits on the edge, raising his shirt sleeve to show his wrist. "You see this bracelet, the one that matches yours?" His eyes lock on mine. "It's a friendship bracelet of sorts." He lets out a small chuckle. "They are linked together. It does more than just track your where-abouts. The moment this bracelet detects that I no longer have a heartbeat, yours will send that powerful bolt of electricity surging through your body." He stands, holding his hands out at his sides. "I die, you die."

I look down at the shiny metal band on my wrist and wonder if he's telling the truth. There's only one way to find out. I bite my tongue and grit my teeth together.

Someone knocks on the door. "Come in," Miles shouts.

One of the guards peeks his head in. "Sir, we need to talk with you."

He looks at me. "Don't try anything. I'll be right

outside that door," he says as he passes me with a slap on my back. I turn my head and watch him walk out, closing the door behind him.

The second the door is closed I stand and move around the desk. I have no idea what I'm looking for, but I won't find anything that can help me if I don't look. I keep close watch on the door while I rummage through the desk, listening intently to their muffled voices.

I open a drawer with my good hand and find his cell phone. I pull it out and quickly type out a text to Jake. "*Stand by Me* in Chicago. Do Not Reply." I hit send and watch as the text goes through, then quickly delete the conversation before putting the phone back and moving on.

I open the next drawer and find a gun. That would come in handy if I were trying to kill the son of a bitch, but I can't do that yet. I slide the gun forward and uncover a black metal box behind it. I pick up the box and it opens with a click. Inside is a foam lining that holds bullets. The tip looks just like a regular bullet, but why would they be in this fancy case? I pick one up and instantly see the difference. The end is in a star shape. These are the nanotechnology bullets I overheard Miles talking about. There is only one bullet missing. I instinctively rub the scar on my chest.

The voices outside of the door grow louder and I see the handle turn just a bit. I snatch a bullet and put the case back, shutting the drawer as I stealthily slide the bullet into my pocket and sit in my chair before the door opens. My heart is pounding from the adrenaline that pulses through my veins and my chest is practically heaving.

I force myself to calm down. One look at me and Miles will know something is up. I hear his muffled footsteps on the carpet getting closer and closer to me. I slow my breathing to a pace that won't arouse his suspicion, even though it makes me want to gasp for air.

"Well, what do you say we get started, John?"

I nod curtly and stand.

As he leads me back to the door, I get a glimpse out the window and know exactly where we are. We're at an old facility that used to house industrial-sized oil drums. That's why I thought I smelled gasoline. My apartment is only a few blocks from here.

I squeeze my hands into tight fists as I push down the urge to kill Miles and his men.

I'm taken into a room that looks like a loading dock. Big garage doors line one wall where semi-trucks would come to unload. On the far side of the room, I see targets lined up against the wall.

I'm nudged on the back to go down the steps to the main landing. Miles remains up on the stairs while both guards stand at my side.

"Are you sure about this?" the guard asks Miles.

I don't hear his reply but the guard hands me the gun. I take the cold metal in my hands, the object almost feeling foreign to me after all this time, and do a press check to make sure the gun is loaded.

It is.

I aim at the target and pull the trigger. The sound of the gun echoes around the room, causing my ears to ring, but I ignore it. I keep shooting until the chamber is empty and I have nothing left to shoot. Squeezing the trigger sent searing pains through my hand, but I don't want to show any outward signs of distress to them.

Everyone turns to look at Miles. He nods one of the guards on, who walks to the far end of the room and retrieves the target. He holds the paper up, showing one big hole in the center of it.

I hit my mark every time.

Miles laughs, the sound echoing menacingly throughout the empty room.

"Next," he says, clapping his hands together like an excited child about to go on a thrill ride.

The guard takes the gun from me and replaces it with a sniper rifle.

Holding the machinery in my grip makes me want to smile, but I hold it back. It's good to be home. I love the power that I feel when I hold a gun like this. Two years ago, I didn't get this rush anymore, but it's been so long since I've been here that I get that same thrill I got when I first took this job.

I take my position and aim at the next target. The distance isn't nearly far enough. I'm used to doing this from hundreds of feet away. I could clearly see the target without the scope, but now, it's just cheating.

I pull the trigger repeatedly and empty the weapon. When I can no longer fire off shots, I hand over the rifle and the guard fetches the target.

Perfect shot every time.

I look at Miles. "Are we good here?" I clinch my jaw as my hand spasms.

He grins. "Yeah, we're good. We're real good."

One guard stays behind to pack up the weapons while the other escorts me back to Miles' office.

When Miles and I are alone, he opens the case on his desk and pulls out two cigars. He hands one to me and lights his own. I've never been much of a smoker, but I take the olive branch that's offered.

I light the cigar and wait to hear my fate.

He pours two glasses of bourbon and slides one across the desk to me. I take it and swirl the liquid. God, it's been so long. My mouth waters just from looking at the amber liquid.

There is a long, awkward silence as he sips his drink and takes a couple puffs off his cigar. Finally, he looks at me. "I have a few jobs that I'm entrusting you with before I give you the motherload. If you can handle these smaller jobs and restore the faith I've lost in you, when you complete the big job, you're free to go. Your debt will be paid."

I can't take it anymore. I throw back the liquid and swallow it. It burns its way down my parched throat and warms my stomach. Deciding to see how far I can push my luck, I stand with my empty glass in hand. I slowly take the few steps to the drink cart and pour another. I drink it while still holding the bottle. When the second drink is gone, I pour another, all while feeling Miles watching me.

I take the third glass and sit back down. "So, let me make sure I have this right. You've been torturing me until I agreed to work for you again, and now you're just going to let me go when I finish this job?"

He looks me square in the eye "If you don't end up dead. This job, it's not like the little shit you did in the past." He takes a draw off his cigar, blowing out a puff of smoke. "I'm afraid that even you can't pull this one off," he says with a grin.

I scoff. "What's the job?"

He seems taken back. "You think I'm going to fall for that shit again?" He shakes his head. "Not this time, John. This time," he says as he leans forward in his leather desk chair which creaks with his movements, "*this* time, we play by my rules. You will not go rogue." He points at his chest with his cigar.

I stub out my cigar and lean back in my chair. "How's this going to play out, huh? You keep me locked up in your dungeon, only letting me out to do your bidding like I'm your little minion?"

He lets out a laugh. "You *are* my little minion, John. The sooner you learn that, the better." As if on key, a guard grabs me by my arm while the other pulls the black bag over my head.

———

WHEN THE SUN RISES, I'M DRAGGED OUT OF BED AND up to the kitchen area they have made on the office floor. Next to my plate of scrambled eggs and sausage is a file.

A file that seals someone's fate.

I take my seat and flip through it while I'm eating. The hit is on a man named Clay Charleston. I study his pictures, memorizing the details of my target. He looks like your typical rich prick to me: slicked-back blond hair, dark eyes, and weak facial features.

I move on to read the papers enclosed. Mr. Charleston was the primary account holder for one Mrs. Betty Charleston. It appears that the day Mrs. Charleston died, the money mysteriously came up missing. The family hired a private investigator and all signs point to her nephew, Clay.

This I can handle. A thief? I've taken out many. Something tells me that Miles is breaking me in slowly.

———

I'M UP ON THE ROOF DRESSED IN MY BLACK GEAR. THE wind is cold and frigid as it nips at my nose and dries my eyes. It's nearing 11 P.M., the time Mr. Clay usually strolls in from his bar crawl.

I adjust my position and peer through my scope just as a nicely-dressed man rounds the corner. I study his face: same preppy haircut as the guy in the picture, same beady little eyes, and pointy nose.

Same class ring on his right ring finger. This is my guy.

I aim for his head and take a deep breath to steady myself. As I exhale, I squeeze the trigger and the gun fires quietly through the silencer.

He drops dead on the sidewalk. Nobody is even around to scream.

I pack up quickly and head back down the fire escape. I walk down the alley at a normal pace, not wanting to draw attention to myself in case someone happens to see me. My ride waits for me around the corner: both guards in the black Hummer.

The guard in the driver's seat shifts into drive immediately after I land in the seat, screeching the tires off the pavement.

When we come to a stop sign, they look down the road and see the man lying still on the sidewalk. They slowly drive past him, turning their heads as they go to make sure he is dead. By the way the blood is pooling around his head, there's no way he can't be.

"Good job, John," one of them says before pulling out a cell phone and reporting the accident. I hear the operator ask for his name, but he closes the phone and throws it out the window.

I sit back and wait to be thrown back in my cell. Job one: completed.

CHAPTER FIVE

Brooklyn

I haven't slept a wink since Jake read the message on the burner phone. It can't be him. He died in my arms. I know Jake says no one else has that number, but Miles' men are capable of anything. The little Napoleon got away. I knew at some point the slimy bastard would resurface. He took my heart from me, what more could he want? But why now? It's been two years, surely he's found someone else's life to ruin.

But, what if?

What if...he's still alive? He wouldn't have stayed away from me. He couldn't. His fierce love for me wouldn't allow it. He was my hero in the shadows, my lover, and my life.

I throw the sheets back, giving up on any thought of sleep. I pull on my silk robe, tying it tightly around my waist. My reflection in the Queen Ann-style floor mirror stops me. I stare at the woman staring back at me. My red locks are longer than the last time I laid eyes on John. My hips and breasts are curvier, thanks to motherhood. I pull back the front of my robe, exposing my thighs. These are the same. The same long thighs that I wrapped around him, holding him close to me, drawing him in as he thrust inside me.

I watch as my fingers impulsively brush the inside of my thigh. I used to love when his teeth nipped me here. I cock my head to the side, eyes fixated on the point of contact between my fingers and skin. My gaze lifts higher as I visualize him on his knees in front of me. His head tilts upward, reading my dark eyes, watching them fill with lust. A sexy smile crosses his face as he leans forward. His smile ceases as his lips touch me and his tongue darts inside. My breathing speeds up as my fingers skim over the junction between my legs through my silk panties. It's not my touch I'm feeling. It's his.

I let my eyes close, picturing him kneeling before me. His back muscles flex while he brings me to the brink of shattering. I can smell him like he's really here. I can feel his heat, an overpowering mixture of love and wanting. It washes over me as I slide my fingers beneath the thin material.

My lips part and a soft moan escapes my lips. I note his cocky grin when he feels how wet I am for him. His eyes darken before his Adam's apple bobs and his jaw flexes. I can see how turned on he is just from pleasuring me.

My fingers work quicker, needing to find my release. My head falls back as my breathing amplifies further and every muscle in my body hardens, preparing for my orgasm. I look at John one last time as my climax washes over me.

"Brook! Are you up?" I jump as Jake's voice brings me back to the here and now, shattering my vision. I scan the mirror for John again, but he's gone. For one blessed moment he was here with me. I fix my robe, drawing it in even tighter this time.

"Brook! Are you in there?" His knock sounds like thunder.

I almost crash into him when I open the door. "I'm here. What's wrong?"

He rushes past me and starts rifling through drawers, throwing clothes on the bed. "Call the Nanny for
J-Man. Get your things packed," he barks at me.

I grab his arm to stop him. "Slow down. What are
you ranting about?" His eyes are grave, filled with a
seriousness I have never before seen in him.

"We're going to Chicago," he says flatly.

"What? Why? I don't want to go back there." I plop
down on the end of my bed, crossing my arms over
my chest.

Jake pulls the burner phone out of his pocket and
squats down in front of me. "I got another text." He
tries to hand me the phone, and I push it away.

"It's Miles playing mind games with us. We talked
about this yesterday." I try to stand but he places his
hands on my knees, keeping me in place.

"I know we did, but I've thought about nothing else
all night long. There is no way Miles has this
number. Think about it. He is more than capable of
getting my cell phone number if he wanted it. Only
John knew I had this phone. I didn't tell another
soul. So, if Miles wanted me or you, the text would

not come to this phone." He holds it in front of me again. "Look at the text."

My hand trembles as I take it from him. There, in big bold letters, it says "*Stand By Me* in Chicago, do not reply." I stand and throw the phone, shattering the mirror that I just saw him in. Jake stands and his hands firmly grasp my shoulders.

"Listen to me. This is John, I know it. We have to go to Chicago and find him." His voice is full of conviction.

"I saw him die! *You* saw him die!" My eyes plead with him to not dredge this up again. I try to walk away but his grip tightens.

"Maybe we saw what Miles wanted us to see. You know what he's capable of, you said it yourself. I know this is John sending these messages. I can feel it, right here." His hand lands over his heart.

I pull out of his reach. "Then where the hell has he been the last two years?" I scream as the floodgates of tears open up. I turn my back to him.

He moves closer to me. "Maybe he's been keeping us safe," he whispers.

I turn to face him. My lip begins to quiver. "Do you honestly think there is a chance that he is alive?"

"I do. I didn't, but now," he picks the phone up off the floor, "I do. And, if there is the slightest possibility that he is alive, I'm going after him. He would do the same for us."

I wipe my tears with both hands, then take the phone out of his hand. I stare at the message again like it's going to start talking to me in John's voice. "I trust you with my life, even with J-Man's life, and if you really think that John is in Chicago, then that's where we will go."

"I do." His eyes scan back and forth over mine, trying to decide if I honestly believe him.

"Then what are we waiting for? I'll clean up this mess, then call the nanny and start packing. You make the arrangements. I'll make a few quick phone calls..."

His hands go to either side of my face. "Thank you, Brook, for trusting me." He kisses my forehead.

The next two hours are a whirlwind. I've not had time to catch my breath, to digest what we are doing.

The nanny, Grace, is staying at our house with John. He will be safe there. Jake installed security cameras and silent alarms when I bought the place. There is a hidden safe room tucked away in John's room. Grace is the only other person besides us that has access to it.

———————

I SHOVE MY OVERSTUFFED LUGGAGE INTO THE overhead bin on the plane. "Jake, I need to call my dad before the plane takes off."

"Don't call him yet, not until we know anything for certain."

"I won't mention John, but I want him to know we are traveling in case something happens." He nods in understanding and I dial his number while I buckle into my seat.

"Hey, Brooky." His voice is always so comforting to me.

"Hi, Dad. I wanted you to know that Jake and I are taking a little trip to Chicago. Little John is with Grace."

"What's in Chicago?" Concern radiates through his voice. He knows I haven't been back there since John died.

"I..." I cover the phone with my hand, "I hate lying to him," I say to Jake.

"I still have my apartment there. I'm going to finish cleaning it out and then Jake and I are going to a baseball game while we are there." I close my eyes tight, waiting for his response.

"I think it's about time that you got rid of that place. You've been holding onto it for far too long. You need the last bit of closure. Tell Jake I said hello and to take care of my little girl."

"I will. I'll call you when we're on our way home. Bye, Daddy."

"I'll come see you soon, Brooky."

"You didn't really lie to him. We are going to your apartment while we are there," Jake says, shrugging his shoulders.

"It was still a lie. If he thought John was still alive, he'd have the FBI looking for him." I turn in his direction in the tight confines of my seat. "Why aren't we getting his help? And why aren't we flying first class?" I yank at my seatbelt.

"This was the only flight out on such short notice and there were no other seats available. We got the last two. To answer your other question, we don't know what kind of trouble we're walking into. I don't want your dad involved."

"Exactly. If we are walking into trouble, then the FBI should be involved." My voice starts to rise.

"Lower your voice. People are starting to stare."

He's right. All eyes are on me as I look around the plane. A few people recognize me and start whispering and pointing at me. "I'm sorry. I just don't understand why we need to do this alone," I whisper.

"My gut tells me not to get other people involved yet," he says, peering out the small oval window.

"Your gut. That's all you got?" I turn his chin toward me.

"I promise we'll ask for help when and if we need it. In the meantime, it's you and me. Okay?"

I let out a deep sigh. "Okay. Where do we start?"

"We'll start at your apartment. We need to go to places that are familiar to him. We may not have to find him."

"What do you mean?"

"He may find us. Where are some other places he knows?"

The plane starts making its decent down the runaway and I grip the armrest anxiously. "John knows the entire city like the back of his hand."

"I want to know where he has been with you."

"There is the bar where we first met." I smile at the memory of that night. "There is the hangar where we spent the night." My smile fades thinking back to where I first realized how much danger I was in and the fact that John became my hero that day. He saved me every day from that point on.

His hand covers mine. "That's good, Brook. Those are places to start. If he's alive, we'll find him."

"I hope to God you are right. The thought of getting my hopes up... I don't know if I can do it again," I say softly.

"I'm sorry. I'm not trying to get your hopes up. I really believe it was him that sent the text." His brows furrow together as he looks away.

"What is it?" I squeeze his hand to get him to look at me.

"I'm his twin. Shouldn't I have known if he was still alive?"

I lay my head on his shoulder. "I don't think it really works that way."

CHAPTER SIX

John

The sound of the heavy door scraping against the floor as it's pushed open wakes me, the same annoying sound that woke me yesterday. Even the dim lights filtering in from the hallway are enough to make me squint.

"Good job, John. I knew you still had it in you," Miles says as he walks deeper into my cell. He reaches above his head and turns on the light, something I don't even bother with anymore. "Get up and shower off. I have a little surprise for you."

I sit up and my overgrown hair falls in my eyes. I push it back as I stand. "What surprise?"

"It wouldn't be much of a surprise if I told you, now would it?"

He turns sideways so I can pass by him to go shower. "When you finish, get your ass upstairs. Don't make me regret this small freedom I'm offering you."

I grunt in response. Walking out of my cell without a guard on my arm brings about a small sense of freedom. I open the door on my right and step into the tiny, dingy bathroom. Clean clothes are set out on the back of the toilet for me, shampoo/body wash is already in the shower, and a towel is hanging on the wall. Shaving cream, a razor, and scissors are waiting for me on the sink. I'd love to pick them up and jab them into his stomach, gutting him like a pig. I snicker to myself at the thought. It's not my style though, I'd much prefer to have a bullet slice through him.

Something feels weird here. Miles is being too nice. But maybe this is another one of his tests. I have to earn his trust back if I'm ever going to get away from him. He may say that if I can pull off this big job that I will be set free, but I don't believe him. If I get away, it's going to be because I got myself out, not because he let me go.

I strip off my clothes and step into the shower. The water takes forever to get warm, but it finally heats up and soothes the sore muscles of my back. I've been using every last minute I have in my cell to exercise. I need to be in shape if I'm going to be out there doing this job again. Between the sit ups, pushups, lunges, and squats, every one of my muscles are sore and tense, but I feel good, stronger.

When I step out of the shower, I take my sweet time shaving and cutting my hair. With the scruff on my face gone and my hair trimmed back into its normal style, I finally look like myself again. All but the ugly scar that mars my cheek. It's jagged and raised, and two inches long.

I pull on the black clothes that were set out for me and slip the bullet I stole from Miles into my boot before making my way up the stairs, surprised still that I don't have a guard watching my every move. I know they are going to pat me down to be sure I don't have anything on me that could be used as a weapon. As I walk toward the stairs, the bullet digs into my calf from my boot being tied so tight, but I ignore the slight irritation.

Miles is waiting for me behind the door to the kitchen area, sitting down at the table while the two guards stand, pacing the floor.

They watch me as I walk across the floor and take a seat, looking at Miles.

"See, everything is fine," he says to his guards. He looks at me. "They were sure you managed to break free while you were down there alone." One of them pats me down to make sure I didn't keep any of the sharp objects they left out for me.

I eye the guards before turning back to Miles. "Why would I do that? You know where to find me. Not to mention the threat you put against my family." Anger washes over me again. It rises in my chest, bringing up bile, but I push it down.

"That's what I said!" he says with a laugh as he motions toward me. His happy go lucky attitude pisses me off more than anything. He has held me captive for two years, tortured me, and threatened my family, but this is all just a good time to him.

"Anyway, let's eat while we talk about this next case." Miles motions toward the guard and he sets down a plate in front of each of us.

I take a sip of coffee and watch as he opens a file and hands over a picture.

I pick the picture up off the table and study it. It's a man that looks to be in his sixties. His graying hair is balding on top. But he has kind blue eyes and a wide smile. He reminds me of my grandpa in this picture. Two young children, whom I assume to be his grandchildren, are sitting in his lap. They all look happy sitting in front of Cinderella's Castle at Disney World.

"What did he do?" I ask.

His dark eyes study me while a smile plays on his lips. "Nothing."

I let the picture fall from my fingers. "Nothing?"

He nods. "That's right. This man hasn't done a damn thing other than work hard and make a lot of money. His beneficiary is getting impatient."

I grit my teeth. "So you're telling me that I have to kill an innocent man so someone can collect on his life insurance?"

He picks up his coffee and takes a sip. "That's right, John."

I take a deep breath and shake my head. I knew this was how it was going to go. He's breaking me in easy. He knew I wouldn't be okay with killing an innocent person. He could have had any of his other lackeys do this job, but this is my test, just another form of torture.

"And if I don't do it?"

He lifts one shoulder and lets it fall while picking up his coffee cup. "Well then, I'd say our fun is over. If you can't pass your tests, you won't get your key to freedom."

Fuck. What choice to do I have?

He must see me waiver because he hands me a map. "Your position will be here." He points to a location on the map. "You'll be going at this solo. No guards. I have to see if I can trust you to get the job done and come back without being supervised. Do you think you can handle that?"

I bite my tongue and nod once while keeping my eyes on my untouched plate of food. I reach down and take the bullet out of my boot and slide it into my pocket.

"Let's get to it then!"

————

I TAKE MY PLACE ON TOP OF THE BUILDING AND DUCK down below the ledge. I have to give Miles credit he's doing everything he can to make this harder with each job. The first was a piece of cake: dead of night, taking out a criminal. This one: middle of the day, busy street, innocent person.

I take a deep breath and peek over the ledge and into the window of my target's office. He has his back turned to the window as he sits at his desk. This is too easy. He's not going to expect it, nor will he feel a thing. It will be over before it even started for him.

I aim my rifle at his head and take a deep breath. He's in my sights, but something is stopping my finger from pulling the trigger. I can't do this. I can't kill an innocent person. I pull my weapon back and lean my back against the ledge, sitting down.

I have to do this. If I don't, I won't ever gain his trust enough to get away. If I fail, he will go after my family.

Images of Brooklyn, Jake, and my son flash before my eyes. That's all I need.

I get back up to my knees and aim the rifle at his head. It's a clean shot, nothing in the way. I take a deep breath and close my eyes, slowly squeezing the trigger.

The rifle fires and I open my eyes to see the man slumped over his desk with blood pooling around him. The computer screen in front of him is shattered and covered in his blood. My stomach rolls and threatens to empty itself... not at the sight of blood, but from killing an innocent man, something I promised myself I would never do. But what choice did I have? I will do anything to keep my family safe. I force myself to pack up my supplies and make my way to the street.

I hop on the bike I was given to complete the assignment and rev the engine, shifting it into gear and peeling out in the direction of my prison, returning like a good little minion.

Job two: completed

––––––––

"Good job, John!" Miles says as I throw down my bag and sit at the table.

"I need a drink."

He stands and opens a cabinet. He pulls out a bottle of bourbon and pours it into a plastic cup before handing it over.

I throw the drink back as quickly as I can and motion for another.

He pours a little more and says, "Now, now, John. Take it easy. There's a reason you did this job in the middle of the day."

"Yeah? Why's that? More people to catch me?"

He lets a small laugh fall from his lips. "No, because your final trial is tonight."

"Two hits in one day?"

He nods as he puts the bottle away and takes his place across from me. "That's right." He pulls out another file.

I set my cup down and watch him open the file and hand me a picture. My heart pounds and my anger skyrockets as I see the Polaroid image of the woman.

"Is this some kind of sick joke?" I ask, not taking my eyes off the photo. The woman looks very similar to Brooklyn with her red curls blowing wildly in the wind. Her eyes are closed, but her smile is wide. Her face shape is nothing like Brooklyn's, it's more rounded than angular. But it doesn't make it any easier. I've never killed women, especially not one that looks like the woman I'm desperately in love with.

He grins. "No joke. Her name is--"

"I don't care," I interrupt. If I have to kill this woman, I don't want to know anything about her. Knowing her will only make this harder.

"Her name is Stacy and she's a kindergarten teacher."

I slam my palm down forcefully on the table, rattling everything on top. "I don't want to hear it."

He doesn't stop. He continues to torture me. "She just got home from her honeymoon. She'll never see it coming."

I stand and flip the table on its side. The contents fly across the room and shatter on impact. The guards make a move toward me, but Miles holds up his hand, stopping them while he sits in the chair as if the table is still there. "I watched your every move on that last job. I saw the way you faltered, only deciding at the last minute to do your job." He stands and walks closer to me. "That's exactly the kind of shit we don't need. I need you to be sure of yourself and the job you're doing. Get out of your fucking head if you ever want to see that little family of yours." He turns and walks away. "The map is in the file. Don't make me regret this."

I lean against the wall and bang my head a few times. I have to get my shit together. I have to get this done if I ever want to be rid of him, if I ever want to see Brooklyn again and meet my son.

After a few quiet minutes of seething to myself. I bend down and pick up the file before moving to sit on the couch. Both guards followed Miles out the paper-covered doors, but I'm sure they're not far away.

I look over the map and see he has me marked to set up around the corner from my apartment building. The mother fucker is just trying to make this hard for me. He's giving me more space and getting me closer to familiar things just to see if I will run.

I look closer and realize that the building I'm supposed to perch upon is the bar that Brooklyn and I met that night so long ago. Memories wash over me of that evening: her blonde wig, that sexy-as-hell black dress that I later peeled off to discover her soft, cream colored skin that teases every inch of me to this very day. If I would have never met her, would she have ended up as one of my hits? The thought of her dying at my hands is chilling.

I shake my head, clearing it of the images.

"Just a little while longer, Brook. Please, don't give up on me," I whisper.

———

I HOP RELUCTANTLY ON THE MOTORCYCLE THAT MILES supplied me and drive the short distance to the bar. I park in the back alley, next to a dumpster, hidden away in the shadows. With my bag slung over my shoulder, I dismount and step back to look up at the tall building.

This building has at least twenty floors, but only the

bottom level is used as the bar. The rest is just unused space, storage.

My eyes land on a fire escape, but it seems to only be accessible from the third floor - which means that I have to walk through the bar undetected. I kick at the small pieces of gravel and curse under my breath. Miles did this shit on purpose, I'm sure of it.

I walk over to the back door and try the handle, but it's locked. Of course it's fucking locked. If I had all my gear, this would be no problem, but Miles didn't give me anything but a gun.

I kick it with the toe of my boot, annoyed by the situation already.

I walk around to the side of the building and in through the front entrance. The black hat I'm wearing is pulled low over my face, hiding my features as much as possible. I've been in this bar so many times, I know exactly how to get to the third floor even though it's clearly marked off.

The bar is in full swing, same as the night Brooklyn and I met here. Multicolored lights flash through the smoky scene while blissful people on the dance floor sway and grind against each other. The music is loud enough and the lights are low enough, I hope, to let me sneak through the crowd unnoticed.

I make my way through the drove of people and slip down the hallway where the bathrooms are located. At the end of the hall is a door - it that leads to the stairs. I keep my head low as I walk quickly down the long, dark hallway. The handle is locked... I'll just have to bust through it. It probably will be inaudible over the music anyway.

I take a step back, ready to ram my shoulder into the door when I hear, "John?"

I freeze. I know that voice. My heart slams against my chest as goosebumps rise on my flesh.

"Is that you?" she whispers, warily taking a few small, slow steps closer.

I want nothing more than to throw her against this wall and kiss her like I've been dying to for two years, but should I do that? Letting her know that it really is me will open a whole different world for her.

I'm still standing with my back turned partially toward her, but when she places her hand on my shoulder, I lose all self-control.

I spin her around, shoving her against the wall. My fingers tangle into her red locks even though my hand protests in pain. I move my lips to hers. I need to feel her, taste her. The moment we touch, she knows it's me. She kisses me back fiercely, running her hands over my face like she can't believe I'm standing right in front of her.

Her delicious scent and sweet taste tease me, making me forget everything else going on around me. I hear a soft moan leave her as I gently bite her lower lip before pulling away.

I pull my head back and hold her to me. "What are you doing here? It's too dangerous." I rest my forehead against hers and close my eyes, fully alive in this short moment together.

"The... the text."

I open my eyes and see hers are brimming with tears. "That was for Jake. Please tell me you didn't come alone."

She shakes her head. "No, he's here with me. We thought you were dead. You've been gone so long," she cries.

"I know. Shh, please don't cry. We don't have time. You need to get out of here." I take a step back, releasing her.

"No! Not without you. How is any of this even possible?" She closes the distance between us again, pulling herself against my chest.

I tilt her head back to look at me. "I can't. Not yet. Miles is watching me. I don't have time to explain. I'm here to complete a job. I don't know what he has up his sleeve for me, but it's dangerous. I need you to take this." I slide my hand into my pocket and pull out the bullet. "See what you can find out about it. It's some kind of nanotechnology."

She takes the bullet and nods.

I lean in and give her one last long, slow kiss. I let her taste sink into me, knowing full well it may be the last.

CHAPTER SEVEN

John

"Go back to Jake. Tell him to keep his phone close by. Get that bullet analyzed. I'll find a way to call him. As soon as I know it's safe, I'll come back to you." I run my hand down her arm, feeling the electrical current coursing through her body.

"Wait! I have so much to tell you, and a million questions," she says as her tears finally fall.

"Please, go." My own words hurt coming out. I need her to get the hell out of here. "*Now*, Brooklyn!" I bark, instantly feeling like a complete asshole. All I want to do is feel her underneath me, but instead I'm causing her more heartache. I watch her walk off into the darkness of the bar. Every ounce of me wants to go after her, but Miles's voice resounds in my mind. *"I'll kill your family."*

I step back, then slam my left shoulder into the door. It doesn't open, but breaks enough that I can jar it open. I rush up the stairs two at a time until I reach the third floor. I sit with my back against the wall under the window, waiting for my heart to slow its breakneck pace. Adrenaline has nothing to do with its pounding this time around; it is entirely from seeing Brooklyn. For a split second, my world was right again. I had her warm body next to mine. I rub my lips together to soak in the taste of her. She is my sole purpose in finishing this mission.

I get up on my knees, assembling my gun with its silencer. I look through the scope for my target. There she stands, sipping a glass of red wine, cutting up vegetables at the kitchen bar. She's beautiful and looks just like Brooklyn. Her bastard of a new husband is the one who put a hit out on her. She inherited a shitload of money from her family and he wants it all for himself. The file indicated that he was the one that killed her family, but she is entirely naïve about his true nature.

My finger rests on the trigger. She looks up at that moment as if she sees me. My hand trembles and sweat beads down my face. My stomach turns. Sitting back down, I take my hat off and wipe my brow with my forearm. I breathe in deeply a few times to keep from hurling.

I can't do this. Not even for Brooklyn. There has to be another way. "Think, Goddamn it, *think*." I beat the back of my head on the wall behind me. "I've got to get her out of there." I pull my hat on and jump off the ground, putting my gun in the back of my pants. I head down the same way I came in and scan the dark bar. My eyes stop in the very back corner. The lighting is dim, but I would recognize her anywhere. She's in Jake's arms crying. I watch her shoulders and head bob slightly in his arms. He's kissing the top of her head.

I take one step toward them and stop myself. She and my son have Jake. They've all survived and they'll do it again. I have to put a stop to this. "Goodbye, Brooklyn," I whisper to myself. She looks up at that moment and I could swear her eyes lock on mine, but there is no time for emotions right now. I force myself to look away and make my escape out of the bar.

Once I clear the door, I rush across the street, darting in between cars. Entering her apartment building, I find the stairs and make my way up quickly. My head is throbbing and sweat continues to roll down my face. I make it to outside her apartment door and turn the knob slowly. It's unlocked.

I walk through the large open living room to the kitchen. She jumps back, holding the knife in the air when she sees me. I raise my hands so that she can see I'm unarmed. "I'm not here to hurt you. Your husband has hired some really bad men to kill you. You need to get out of here."

"Get out of my house!" she screams and moves toward her cell phone sitting on the kitchen counter.

I pull my gun out, aiming it at her. She drops the chopping knife and it clangs on the tile floor. "I don't want to hurt you, Stacy."

"How do you know my name?" her voice quivers and she visibly shakes with fear.

"I don't have time to tell you everything, but you need to leave now or your life will end today."

Her body stills and she takes a step toward me. "My husband wouldn't do such a thing." I watch her hand as it runs across the countertop, moving closer to me. My hand shakes and my eyes blur as the sweat pours down my face. Why the fuck isn't she running?

"You're scared," she says, stepping even closer.

"If you won't leave, I will kill you. I don't have any other choice." I lean my head to one side, cracking my neck, trying to regain control.

"Then you will have to kill me."

"Just fucking leave! Please... please don't make me do this." She stands her ground in front of me. My finger moves to the trigger. I close my eyes for a split second and see Brooklyn's face. My mind flashes forward to when she learns what I've done to get back to her. The disgust and hate in her eyes is more than I can bear. I can't live with her hating me and I can't live the rest of my life doing Miles' dirty work.

I exhale loudly and slam the gun on the counter. "I'm telling you the truth. Your husband wants you dead so that he can have all the money you inherited!" I step backward out into the living room. She grabs the gun off the counter and follows me. "*He* is the one that killed your family. He made it look like an accident."

"I know what my husband is up to." Suddenly she looks nothing like Brooklyn. The innocent face of a teacher has turned into a killer. Her hand is steady as she points the gun at me. "I learned of my husband's actions on our honeymoon." She saunters closer. "I guess Miles forgot to change the name in the contract to my husband as the mark. I'll have to make sure to get my money back." She spits out the '*k*' as she speaks.

"Go ahead, kill me. I'm a dead man either way. I deserve to die for the things that I've done. I'm no better than the man that employs me." I drop to my knees and lower my head. "When this is over, you'll meet a woman named Brooklyn." I raise my eyes to hers. "Tell her I'm sorry and that I love her more than life itself."

She steps closer to me and lets out a snicker. "Do it, please. I'm begging you to put me out of my misery." I lower my head again and then I hear a crash.

Brooklyn is on top of her, wrestling her for the gun. A porcelain vase lays in pieces on the floor. It slices into Stacy's arm as she struggles for control. "Brooklyn, no!" I yell and move toward her, but my feet become cemented in place at the sound of a gunshot. I see the recoil of the gun jerking between their bodies, and then it's flung under the coffee table. My ears ring from the loud explosion in the small apartment, and the smell of gunpowder burns my nose. The bullet miraculously shoots out from between them, shattering a glass picture frame and disappearing into the drywall.

Stacy rolls Brooklyn beneath her, wrapping her hands around her throat. Brooklyn's face turns red, and her eyes start to roll back. I reach for the gun under the coffee table. I steady my hand and take aim, squeezing the trigger. Stacy immediately slumps over. Brooklyn thrusts the weight of Stacy off her and scrambles into my arms with tears already falling. "She was going to kill you," she cries. "I couldn't watch you die again."

"Why did you follow me? I told you to get away from me." I say the words as I kiss the tears streaming down her face. "Where the hell is Jake?" I say all of this while my hands roam her body. I need to touch her.

"I told him I had to go the bathroom. I saw you in the bar. I recognized that look in your eyes and I had to come after you."

I place my hand on her chin and tip her head up so that I can look at the red marks on her neck. I place my lips tenderly on them and kiss each fingerprint bruise left behind on her creamy skin. I need to get her the hell out of here. "Brooklyn, look at me. You need to leave." I swiftly stand with her. I take her hand and lead her to a bedroom, pulling open several drawers before I find what I need. I throw a shirt at her. "Change into this and give me your shirt."

She looks down for the first time, realizing she has blood splattered on her after the struggle with Stacy. Her skin pales and fear fills her dark eyes. She starts to tremble.

I take her face between my hands and steady her eyes on me. "You didn't do this. I did. This is all my fault."

"Why did you tell her to kill you? What the hell were you doing here in the first place?" The fear in her eyes is replaced by deep anger and her chest swells from trying to contain all her emotions.

"I promise to explain everything later, but you have to get out of here. I need to fix this. Take the bullet I gave you and do as I asked."

"No, I'm not leaving you," she says as she yanks off the blood-stained shirt. She uses it to wipe the crimson from her hands before tossing it to me, then tugs the fresh shirt on and squares her shoulders.

I take her by the arm and lead her to the door. "For the love of God, do as you're told. If you're caught with me, you, Jake, and our son are all dead."

I feel her suddenly put the brakes on. "You know about John?" she gasps.

It takes a split second to register that she named him after me. I pull her into my arms. "Yes, I know about our son. Miles has been threatening me with John. Not just him, my entire family. Now please, do as I ask. Do you remember how to get to the hangar we hid out in?"

She pulls back to look at me. "Yes, I remember."

"You and Jake get to the hangar. Tell Todd I need you hidden. As soon as I can get there, I will. I promise." I can't resist pulling her in for a kiss. She returns my kiss with the same blinding passion that I remember so well. I have to force myself to leave her lips. "Go," I say before watching her walk down the hallway, glancing back at me every few steps.

Before Brooklyn opens the door to the stairwell, she stops and turns, facing me. "I love you," she mouths toward me.

"I love you too, baby," I mouth back.

I run back inside, closing the door behind me. A bottle of Clorox bleach is in the cabinet under the kitchen sink, which I use to quickly wipe down anything Brooklyn might have touched. My gloves will keep all evidence away from me.

The doorknob jiggles behind me, calling my attention. A tall man wearing an expensive suit ducks his head as he walks through the doorway. He sees me and quickly shuts the door behind him. I'm leaning over his dead wife with my hand on the gun lying beside her.

His long, lean face conveys no emotion as he sets his briefcase down beside the couch. He walks over to me and leers. Stacy's eyes are hollow and fixed on the ceiling. "I see that you are very successful at your job." His words are cold as he cocks his head to one side.

I slide the gun up my leg, so that he can't see it, and I slowly stand aiming the gun toward him. "She was totally innocent until you put a mark on her head. You, I have no problem killing." I squeeze the trigger. Shock covers his face as he drops to his knees, then breathes his last breath, falling over next to his dead wife.

Something inside of me feels off. This job never used to bother me this much. But that was before Brooklyn found my heart buried deep under the blood and destruction I had caused. I tear my eyes away from them, no longer able to stomach what I'm seeing. I turn my back and take a deep, cleansing breath. I need to shake this off, I have to get out of here.

I finish wiping everything down and make my way downstairs. I pull my hat lower and dart out the back door. Once I'm far enough away from the building, I take off in a sprint, not stopping until I reach my motorcycle. I slow my pace when I see a familiar dark SUV parked just a few feet away from my bike. I rap my gloved knuckles on the dark tinted window. I'm surprised to see Miles face behind a pair of sunglasses. He never comes near the kills.

"Is the job complete?" he asks, sliding his sunglasses down the bridge of his fat little nose.

"Yes," I answer, looking straight ahead, not wanting to let him see the conflict and anger this job has birthed inside of me. I fall silent, straddling my bike and grabbing my helmet. Before I pull it all the way on, I hear Miles.

"Did you kill both of them?" He flicks a cigarette out the window.

I send my helmet flying to the ground and jerk my leg off the bike. "You fucking bastard." I'm almost to him when he aims a gun out the window at me, laughing.

"When are you going to learn that you are nothing more than a puppet to me? I would think twice about your next move. You are so close to being a free man. I suggest you change your attitude and meet me back at the office." He keeps the gun trained on me as the driver stomps on the gas, squealing the tires on the pavement.

My heart slows to its normal beat. When I saw his face appear from behind the tinted window, I thought he knew Brooklyn had found me. If he did, he would have killed her and thrown her body in front of me. She's safe for now.

CHAPTER EIGHT

John

*N*o one else is in Miles' office when I arrive, so I make myself at home. I help myself to the bottle of bourbon sitting on the cart in the corner, generously filling one of the expensive crystal glasses set next to it. Bourbon in hand, I sit purposely in the leather high-back chair behind his desk, eyeing the pack of cigarettes on the desk. I've never been much of a smoker, but I need something right now to calm my anger.

I pull a cigarette from the pack and place it between my lips, then light the end with the lighter that's lying beside them. The harsh smoke burns deep in my lungs, burning away the sharp edges of my emotions.

Miles knew what he was doing when he sent me on that job. Neither party in that couple was innocent. Innocent people don't put hits out on each other. Hell, I wouldn't put it past Miles to make a deal with both of them just to double his money. He perceived what my reaction would be. He knew I'd have trouble killing that woman, but he also gathered that she would put up a fight. He probably told her husband to go in after he tracked me inside the building. What he didn't plan on, though, was Brooklyn being there. I'm thankful he had no visuals on me during the hit.

Getting myself mixed up in this shit is one thing, but dragging her back into it is another altogether. I wish Jake wouldn't have brought her. As much as I want to see her, I'd rather have her safe and far away from this.

Miles saunters into the office with his two goons on his heels. He snorts when he sees me sitting in his seat, but chooses to ignore it and take the chair across from me. "Well that was a shit show if I ever saw one," he says with a laugh.

I take a drag and blow the cloud of smoke in his face. "Are you going to tell me what the 'big job' is or what?"

He stands and walks to the minibar, pouring himself a drink as he thinks it over. He downs the liquor in several loud gulps and pours another before sitting back down.

"Either tell me so I can get it done or let me the fuck go. I'm ready to get on with my life."

He leans forward in his seat. "This *is* your life, John. Just because you got a glimpse of a normal life doesn't mean it was ever in your reach. You're an assassin, John. And killers don't get happy endings."

Anger rises in my chest and erupts out of me. "Before you, I had never murdered an innocent person!"

He swirls the amber liquid in his glass. "You're not God. You don't get to decide who lives and dies. You've sinned, whether you want to believe it or not. Don't fool yourself into believing that you're some sort of hero here."

He's right. I don't deserve a happy ending. I've killed people. A lot of people. Doesn't matter if they were lower than the scum on the bottom of my boot or not. It wasn't my decision to make, but as long as I believed the world was a better place without them, I didn't give it a second thought. Not until *her* anyway.

Miles laughs. "Don't blame all your problems on me. Do I have to remind you of the skinny kid that came begging to make some real money? Do I need to remind you how you felt when you held that gun in your hands for the first time? Or how about watching the light fade from the eyes of the first life you took?"

I grit my teeth together and flex my jaw trying to keep from strangling the bastard right here and now. A slideshow plays through my mind, showing me the faces of those that I've killed. Every soul I've taken has taken a small piece of my own with it, leaving me with almost nothing left. I'm a monster. I bring nothing but pain and death to every single person I meet. I should have died on that boat two years ago. The world would've been a better place then.

Miles' laugh draws me out of my head. "There's no point in regretting it all now. It can't be changed. We are where we are." He motions toward the guard by the door, who brings over a file. He drops it on the table in front of me.

I look down at it, but don't move to open it. Whatever is in this file will be the hardest thing I have ever had to do.

"Go on. We don't have all night."

I take a deep breath and open the folder. On top of the stack of photos is one of Knox, the man that ordered the hit on Brooklyn.

This triggers a small smile. I'd be more than happy to take this guy out.

"Don't get too excited. Keep looking," Miles says.

I flip to the next picture and my jaw drops. It's Matthew, President Warren. Brooklyn's dad.

"You want me to kill the *President of the United States*?"

An evil smile darkens his face. "That's right."

I close the file, banging my hand against the desk in exasperation with a thud that echoes around the room. "How is Knox putting out a hit from prison?"

He takes a sip of his drink and shrugs. "He has a long reach, much further than you or I."

I finish the liquid in my glass and pour another, filling it to the brim before returning to Miles' chair. "And if I won't do it?"

He leans in, resting his arms on the desk. "Then we'll have a big problem." He stands. "Do I just need to kill you now and send them after your family, because I can do that. No sense in wasting time here."

"No! I'll do it. I just need to make a plan. I mean, how in the fuck am I even going to get close to him?"

He sits back down with a smile, happy to have gotten his way yet again. "If memory serves me correctly, you already have a relationship with him. Use your connections, make him trust you so he will let his guard down."

"You don't think coming back from the dead will raise some red flags?" The cigarette, long forgotten in my hand, has burned its way down to my fingers. I stub it out with a little too much force.

"Well, make your plan and do it fast. I'll be by in the morning to see what you've come up with." He stands and walks to the door. "Make sure you get him back to his cell," he tells the guards with a nod in my direction before stepping from the office.

I need to get out of here and warn him. I know this bracelet can kill me instantly if Miles wishes, but he won't know anything until tomorrow. That will be enough time to get a message out and maybe even see Brooklyn one last time.

I look at the black gear bag from the last hit, unnoticed by the guards and sitting on the floor by the desk. *Huge mistake, Miles,* I think to myself. I have to act quickly.

The guards take several unknowing steps toward me to drag me back to my cell as soon as the door closes behind Miles. I quickly lean down toward the bag.

Realization lights up their faces and they immediately turn tail and sprint to the door. Not fast enough.

The barrel of the gun, silencer still equipped, is aimed directly at them before they have made it halfway across the room. I pull the trigger, dropping the guard on the left like a sack of potatoes. His blood splatters across the door as his partner reaches for the handle. Shocked to see his companion taken, he changes his course back towards me.

He is quick, closing the distance between us in a split second. Operating on autopilot, I swing the barrel in his direction and squeeze the trigger twice before sidestepping his massive body. He lunges past me, loses his balance, and falls to the floor with a look of shock on his face.

I stand panting for a moment with the gun trained on his back, ready in case he jumps back up, but he lies still with his face on the floor. As I watch, a puddle of blood begins pooling out around him, and his heaving chest falls still.

I roll him over to check out the wound. I need him dead. I can't have anyone alerting Miles after I leave. He can't know I'm gone until morning. He's retired for the evening and won't bother checking in until morning.

When I look at him, the light has already faded from his eyes. I check his pulse to be sure, and the soft thumping I should feel beneath his skin is gone. I stand and walk toward the door, stopping to check on the other guard. Nothing. No pulse, no breathing, just lots of blood. I grab my bag and throw it over my shoulder before walking out and hopping on my bike.

I make a quick stop at a gym I used to attend. I rented a locker here to keep a few items stashed away in case I ever found myself in this kind of predicament. I don't have to worry about the locker being reclaimed because the locker rental and gym membership are taken from one of my accounts each month automatically.

Luckily for me, I don't need a key card to get in. I walk in through the doors like I'm just a regular guy here to work out. I make my way into the locker room and walk through until I find the one that belongs to me.

I place my thumb against the fingerprint scanner, causing it to scan my print. The light changes from red to green and it pops open.

I reach in and pull out my black duffle bag. Leaving

the door open, I place the bag on the bench behind me and unzip it to reveal guns, ammo, and enough cash and fake documentation to leave the country.

I close the bag and sling it over my shoulder. It's time to take back what's mine.

———————

I PULL UP TO THE HANGAR WHERE I TOLD BROOKLYN and Jake to go. It's late and no lights are on in the place. I quietly walk up the stairs to the apartment. As I reach my hand towards the door, someone grabs me by the throat and throws me against the outside wall.

It's Jake. Anger is etched on his face until he realizes it's me. "John?" he whispers.

I nod, still unable to talk from the force he's applying to my throat.

I watch as the emotions on his face reverse themselves until he suddenly pulls me in for a hug. "I knew it. I knew we'd find you."

He pulls away with a slap on my back. "God, I'm so glad you're okay." He places his arm around me and leads me in the door.

As soon as my foot is on the carpet, I'm almost knocked over as Brooklyn jumps into my arms, wrapping her legs around my hips and kissing me like she thought she would never be able to again.

I place my hands on her ass to support her weight as I turn and press her against the wall. My lips move with hers as she starts pushing my leather jacket off me.

Jake clears his throat. "Umm...guys?"

I hold up my finger, telling him to wait. I just need a few more seconds to taste her, to feel her. I want nothing more than to ravage her right here. I miss the way she tastes. I miss making her make that little sound that could bring me to my knees. I miss feeling her move beneath me. But there is business to take care of first.

I slowly start to pull myself away as I set her on her feet. Her dark eyes look up at me and she runs her thumb along the scar on my cheek. "Are you okay?"

I nod. "I am for now, but I have some news and I think you both need to take a seat."

The three of us move into the kitchen and Brooklyn and Jake sit at the bar. I reach in the fridge and grab a beer, taking a long drink before beginning.

I look at Brooklyn first. "You need to call your dad and warn him."

"Warn him about what?" Her eyes are wide and full of fear.

"Knox put a hit on him. Miles says that if I follow orders and take him out, that I'll get my life back. That we'll all be free."

"You don't actually believe him, do ya, John?" Jake asks.

I look over at him. "Not in the slightest." I shake my head. "But he needs to be warned because if I don't do it - which I won't," I look back at Brooklyn, "then someone else will try."

"Where ya been all this time? Have you just been running around the city, doing jobs for Miles?" Jake asks, crossing his arms over his broad chest. I just now notice how much weight he's put on. He's finally healthy and has a thick head of dark hair with some gray showing at the temples.

"Not exactly." I lean against the counter and take another swig of my beer. "I've been held captive and sedated a good portion of the time. Miles thought that I would break and come back to work for him."

"For two years?" Brooklyn asks.

"I didn't break until he showed me a picture of the three of you and threatened to kill you all. I couldn't let that happen, so I finally agreed." I start pacing the floor. "He's been putting me through these tests to see if he could trust me. I passed them all. I killed everyone he put in my way to get back to you." I reach out and place my hand on her cheek. "But that's when he told me about your dad."

A sadness covers her face. "What are you going to do? Where does he think you are right now? Will he come looking for you?"

"The problem is... this thing." I hold up my arm, showing them the metal band on my wrist.

"What is that?" Jake asks, moving closer.

"It's linked to Miles. It's a tracker, and up until a few days ago, I wasn't allowed out of the building. But he says it can kill me with the push of a button. If he realizes I'm gone, and he wants me dead, I will be and there won't be a damn thing any of us can do to stop it."

I hear Brook's sudden breath as she covers her mouth.

"Let's get the damn thing off then," Jake says with a shrug.

CHAPTER NINE
John

I flick on the overhead light before we take the stairs down into the hangar. "Todd has to have something here we can use to get this damn thing off," I say as I reach the bottom step. Brooklyn has her hands on my shoulders like she's afraid I will disappear if she's not touching me.

"There's a red tool box in the corner," Jake points at it.

Brooklyn slides her hand in mine as we walk over to it. "I don't see anything in here but a bunch of screwdrivers." They clank together when I move them around.

"Here's a hacksaw," Jake says.

"I'd like to keep my hand attached to my arm, if that's okay with you," I chuckle.

"Will this work?" Brooklyn reaches across me and grabs a pair of bolt cutters.

"This is perfect. God, I love you." I smack my lips to hers and she smiles.

I hand them to Jake and rest my wrist on a metal cabinet. "Baby, look for a hammer or something we can destroy it with once it's off." She starts rummaging through all the different drawers.

Jake places the bracelet between the bolt cutters. "Try not to move."

"One last thing," I say quickly before he can apply pressure.

His eyes pop up to mine. "What's that?"

"There's a small chance that this thing could go off."

He stands up straight, pulling back the bolt cutters. "What do you mean *go off*?"

I shrug one shoulder. "It's supposed to be able to send a powerful bolt of electricity. Sort of like a really fierce shock collar for a dog."

He lifts his eyebrows as he nods his head. "I'm game if you are." He smiles.

I place my hand on his before he squeezes. "I've missed you, man."

"Don't go getting all sappy on me yet. If we don't get your ass out of this, you're still a dead man." He places the bolt cutters on the bracelet and squeezes the two arms together, causing his muscles to bulge through his shirt. At first it only puts a dent in it. He repositions himself and throws all his weight into it, nearly snapping my wrist.

The sharp blades finally slice through the metal bracelet just as a surge of electricity cracks, sending the bolt of lightning through my arm. The bolt cutters conduct the electricity and Jake gets a shock too. We both yell out and fall to our knees with a slight twitch. The bracelet clanks to the floor. The shiny silver metal is now blackened and charred.

"Oh my God! Are you two okay?" Brooklyn rushes over to us.

My whole arm tingles from the current running through it, but luckily we didn't get the full blast of power.

I shake my arm, hoping to regain feeling. "I'm fine. You okay?" I ask Jake.

He nods as he makes his way to his feet, wiping the sweat from his brow. "Yeah, I 'm fine."

"I found a hammer," Brook says holding the hammer up for us to see.

"Do you want to do the honors?" I ask, bending over for the bracelet. It suddenly occurs to me that it may have a little power left in it. I reach out quickly, tapping it to see if I get another shock, but it's spent with nothing left.

I pick it up and hold it out to her.

"Hell yes!" she says, taking it from me and throwing it onto the concrete floor. She squats down and rears back with the hammer, smashing it until it's in several pieces. "That felt good," she says, brushing her hair out of her face with her shoulder.

"That should keep you safe, at least for tonight." Jake picks the pieces off the floor and throws them in the garbage.

"Did you get a chance to do anything with the bullet I gave you?" I say as I pull Brook into my arms.

"No. I have an old friend here in Chicago that can help me. He used to handle some research projects for me when I was in town. I'll see if I can get ahold of him."

"How good of a friend?" I pull her against my chest with my hands on her ass. We're practically nose to nose. I can feel her sweet breath caressing my face. I wet my lips while keeping my eyes locked on hers.

"He's a big, burly guy and weighs about 350lbs. He never leaves his basement. I like my guys a little outdoorsy, so I think you are safe." She laughs. "Oh." She pulls back from me. "I did see a computer upstairs. I wanted to see if I could find any technology on the bullet"

"Why don't you go do that after you call your dad? He needs to be warned as soon as possible. I need to chat with my brother."

"Okay. But Jake, don't let him out of your sight." She points two fingers at his eyes and then back at hers.

"I won't," he laughs out as we watch her walk into the loft. "She's a handful," he says, turning in my direction.

"Don't I know it. Thanks for taking care of her all this time."

"Hell, she took care of me and little John. She's a remarkable woman."

Looking down, I stuff my hands in my pocket and begin rocking my feet back and forth. "Are you... well... did you...?"

He laughs. "I don't think I've ever seen you look more uncomfortable. Spit it out, man."

"Are the two of you together?"

"Oh, God no! What would make you even ask me that?" He looks totally offended.

I take the picture of the three of them out of my pocket and hand it to him. "Miles gave me this."

He takes it out of my hand and looks at it closely. "I could see why maybe you would think that." He puts his hand on my shoulder. "You asked me to look out for her if anything ever happened to you. She ended up taking care of me until she found out she was pregnant. It was the happiest and the saddest moment of her life. I wanted to be an everyday part of hers and your child's life, but she's like a sister to me. Nothing more." The honesty in his eyes burns into me.

I lean back on the cabinet, relief washing over me. "Thank you," I say, looking down at my feet. "How is my son?" I look up and meet his eyes again now that I'm not feeling so insecure.

"He's beautiful. Brooklyn is the most amazing mother. She is so good with him. She tells him stories about you. He thinks you're a superhero, man."

"I can't wait to meet him." I smile just from thinking about the little guy. "Where is he?"

He leans against the table across from me, crossing his arms over his broad chest. "He's with the Nanny, back in Maui."

"You live in Maui?"

"Yeah, Brooklyn said you mentioned something about spending the rest of your lives in Hawaii. She took you seriously. She shut down everything in DC, and told her father she wanted nothing more to do with politics. She went into hiding. This is the only time she's left the island since we moved there. She rides that bike of yours everywhere," he adds.

"And, you're not getting it back either," Brook says, walking toward us.

"I'm alive so I think it's still mine," I tease with her.

"Alive or not, the only time your ass is getting on that bike is if your chest is pressed to my back." She takes a step closer. "Or, if you fuck me on it again." Her arms wrap around my neck as she grins up at me, lust filling her eyes.

"Um... I think that is my cue to leave." Neither one of us acknowledge him as he walks toward the stairs.

That quickly, I'm lost in her. "I've thought about you every day," I tell her between kisses.

"God, I've missed you." Her hands are tugging at my hair.

I put my hands on either side of her face, pulling her closer until we're nose to nose. "I wish there was a better place to make love to you than in here."

"I don't care where it is, as long as you are making love to me."

I step back from her, taking her hand in mine. I walk her over to the small Cessna passenger plane. "Are you a member of the mile-high club?" I tilt my head in the direction of the plane.

"I think that only counts when it's in the air." She laughs, but runs up the narrow metal stairs dragging me with her. She almost bumps her head on the open door. I duck just in time.

I take the passenger seat and slide it back, then pull the door down, closing us inside. When I turn back around, she has stripped down to her black silky underwear. Her eyes are fully dilated and her greedy hands are reaching for my zipper.

"I want you so badly." Her lips are on mine.

"We need to slow down. It's been so long, I don't think I will last," I tell her as she rips my shirt off over my head. My hands find the little strings holding up her panties. I entwine my fingers on either side of them and tear them from her. "Fuck slow." I devour her mouth, then trail kisses down her neck to her shoulder. Her hands are already on my cock, stroking me. I groan and move down her body, kissing and biting every inch of her as I go. She tries to go to her knees with me, but I hold her in place. I want to taste what I've been missing. I want to taste what is mine. I spread her legs wider and my tongue finds its home between her sweet folds. She lets out a sound that lets me know that I am, in fact, right where I belong. Her wetness covers my face as I lick and suck her into my mouth. Her nails dig into my shoulders, egging me on.

My cock is rock hard, but I try to ignore it so that I can have more of her. I tilt my head up to look at her. As I suck her into my mouth, her eyes jump to mine. The heat in her eyes pushes me over the edge. In one swift move, I pull her down onto my lap, placing her entrance over my aching cock.

She slides down easily and I can feel myself begin to throb. "Hold still," I rasp out, keeping her hips from moving. I steady myself for a moment, breathing in and out deeply. I take her nipple into my mouth and suck, then draw it between my teeth. I can already feel her building, the slight squeeze of her muscles gripping around my cock.

"Please let me move," she begs. "I don't care if it's quick. I remember how soon you recover," she says, leaning her head down and biting my shoulder. She rocks her hips back and forth and I can stand no more. I roughly grab her hips with my hands and start a hard, fast rhythm. Her hands press into my shoulders and her head flies back.

She screams my name. "John!"

"Say it again, baby," I grit out between my teeth.

"John!" Her inner muscles squeeze tighter, drawing me deeper inside. I try to hold on a minute longer, but the tingling sensation that moves up my body won't allow it. I hold her tighter to me and come fiercely inside her, letting out a primal sound.

Neither one of us have time to catch our breaths before our need for each other takes over again. This time, I take my time enjoying touching her skin, remembering all of her familiar sounds she makes with each touch. When she can stand no more, she rolls over underneath me and pushes her ass in the air, causing me to move behind her. She places her hands on the seats and shifts her head to look behind her.

Her eyes are dark and her lips are swollen from our kiss. Her hair falls in her face, but I can still see her watching me between the fiery strands. I slip inside her from behind and she rocks back against me. Snaking my hand over her hip and between her legs, I feel for her hard nub, and start rubbing small, firm circles. She starts coming undone as I thrust in and out of her as hard as I can. My skin slaps against her skin, and her head jolts forward with every powerful thrust.

She angles her head to look at me and bites her lip, stifling her scream. It only takes one last, deep thrust before I'm spilling inside of her. We're both too breathless to even move. The windows on the small plane have fogged over, leaving a moisture in the air that clings to our skin. When our breathing and heart rates slow, I pull out of her and sit back, pulling her into my lap. Our bodies are covered in sweat. The plane sways gently beneath us in response to our passionate lovemaking.

When we finally calm, she curls into my arms and lays her head on my chest. Her hand finds the star shaped scar and traces it. "Does it still hurt?" She asks, lifting her head to look at me.

I take her hand and kiss the tips of her fingers. "Just a little."

"When we get you back home, I can take it out."

She takes my hand in hers. "What happened to your hand?"

"I pissed off one of the guards. He stomped on it as one of his buddies held me down."

She kisses the top of my hand softly. "I can take care of this too."

"The only thing I want to do when we get home is make you my wife and make love to you every night. I want to hold my son in my arms and never let him go." I shift her off me and roll to my side to face her. "Tell me about our son."

Her fingers trace my jaw. "He's beautiful and so smart. He talks so well for a fifteen-month old. Jake and I have made a point of not baby talking to him." Her hand moves to my hair. "He looks so much like you."

I lean down and kiss her eyelid. "He has your dark eyes."

"Yes, he does, but everything else about him is you. Even the way he moves. Sometimes I would watch him and I'd see one of your expressions cross his face and I'd have to hold back the tears."

"What else?" My hand traces her belly button.

"He loves to swing. It's his favorite thing to do. Jake bought him this huge outdoor play set. It has a pirate ship in the middle of it."

"I can't wait to be the one that spends time spoiling him, but I have to finish this. First I have to prove Knox put a hit out on your father and then, if it's the last thing I do, I'm going to kill Miles. If I don't, he will always be after us and I refuse to let him anywhere near my family ever again."

"We'll figure out a way together." She licks her lips and then kisses me ever so sweetly.

"You know, I think we made it into that mile high club."

She lays back down, laughing. "How do you figure?"

"I know at some point we were flying."

She rolls back up. "You are so corny. I love you, John."

"I love you, too." I press her shoulder back down. "I'll show you corny." My mouth is on hers again, but our moment is abruptly interrupted by a noise inside the hangar that has me moving to the small oval window in the plane.

CHAPTER TEN

John

I scan the garage but see nothing out of the usual. "Get your clothes back on," I tell Brook while rapidly pulling on my own.

"What did you see?" she asks while tugging her shirt over her head.

"Nothing, but that doesn't mean there isn't anyone out there." I button my jeans and quickly pull on my boots, then open the door to the plane as quietly as possible. "Stay here until I say it's safe," I whisper as I slowly and cautiously make my way out of the plane.

I left the bag with Miles' guns back in the studio apartment. I've left myself completely vulnerable. I grab a heavy wrench off the workbench and hold it at the ready as I make my way around the plane. I have to be quiet and quick. If this is Miles or one of his men, they will be armed and I'll be screwed. I just got her back, I'm not losing her again.

I peek over the row of standing toolboxes and see the top of someone's black hat. I know it's not Jake, he has a head-full of hair, and after being bald for so long, I'm sure he's proud of it and wouldn't dare cover it up.

I turn the corner with the wrench raised above my head, ready to swing if needed. The man turns toward me when I am just a few feet away.

Our eyes meet and the wrench clatters to the ground. "Todd?"

The initial fear in his eyes vanishes, replaced with excitement and confusion. "John?"

A smile spreads across my face as I pull him in for a hug.

He slaps me hard on the back. "Where the hell you been? I thought you were dead."

I pull back and laugh. "I know, I'm sorry. I've just been a little tied up these last couple of years."

The next thing I know, Brooklyn is jumping around the corner with a fire extinguisher held over her head, ready to swing.

I spin around to face her and can't help the laugh that escapes me.

"Oh. It's you," she says, looking at Todd.

I run my hand through my hair. "I thought I told you to stay put?"

She shrugs before handing over the fire extinguisher. "Listening has never been my strong suit." She turns toward Todd and pulls him in for a hug. "Thank you for everything, again. I know we left quite a mess in here the last time we stayed."

When she pulls away, his face is flushing red. As he adjusts his hat, he says, "Well, the place needed a fresh coat of paint and some new carpet. You just gave me the little push I needed to get the work done."

A flashback hits me of the last time we stayed in his apartment: me standing behind the door, Brooklyn standing in the middle of the room looking like a deer in the headlights as one of Miles' men came after us. I can still hear the gunshot ringing in my ears when I pulled the trigger and landed a perfect shot in his temple before he even knew where I was hiding. It seems like it was so long ago, yet just yesterday at the same time.

"I just stopped by to pick up a few tools. I had a buddy of mine call asking for help fixing his plane in the morning."

I shake my head clear of the haunting images running through it. "I'm sorry again," I say, reaching for his hand to shake. "If you'd been through what I have been, you'd be a little jumpy too."

He shakes my hand and slaps me on the bicep with his other. "Don't worry about it, John. I'm just glad you're okay."

"I'll take her upstairs and get out of your hair." I take Brooklyn's hand and lead her back toward the apartment.

"I'll be expecting dinner and drinks when all this settles down for you," Todd shouts back at me.

"Deal! Dinner, drinks, on me. You deserve it after all you've done for us."

We walk into the pitch-dark apartment, greeted by the sound of Jake's deep, even breathing. I pull Brook back against my chest and whisper in her ear. "Take a shower with me?"

She doesn't answer, but I feel her lips graze my neck as she nods her head.

I move my lips to hers and place my hands on her hips, lifting her up against me. She wraps her long legs around me as I carry her to the bathroom.

The bathroom is small - so small that I don't even have to walk, just turn in circles. I bend over, turning on the shower, and then turn back to her so I can place my hands on either side of her face.

"What is it, John?"

I shake my head. "Fuck, you're beautiful," escapes my lips before I lean back in and place a kiss on her collarbone.

My hands find the hem of her shirt and I yank it off over her head while my lips trail across her skin.

She pulls my shirt off before guiding my lips to hers. Her fingertips skim across my chest before she pulls away, deep concern etched on her face.

"What's wrong?" I ask her.

Her soft touch moves from the scar on my chest to the small, circular scars on my biceps and forearms. "What did he do to you?" she asks with tears in her eyes.

I place my hands back on her cheeks and direct her eyes to mine instead of my scarred body. "Nothing I couldn't handle." I shake my head. "Don't look at the ugly marks covering my body. Just look at me. See me. I'm still the same guy you fell in love with."

She bites her lower lip and her eyes fall to the floor. "This is all my fault."

I pick her up and sit with her on my lap with my back pressed against the door. "Nothing is your fault. You didn't do this. Miles is just a sick son of a bitch. This would've happened eventually anyway. You're not to blame here."

"If I wouldn't have created that vaccine, if I hadn't of come to Chicago, none of this would've happened to you. You'd still be living in that penthouse of yours, taking home random girls from the bar." Her lips turn up just a bit from remembering our first night together.

"If I didn't have you, I would've had nothing to get me through these past two years. You are the only thing that got me through. I would've given up long ago. I kept living for you. I held on every day just for you."

She stands and holds out her hand to help me to my feet. "What do you say we get in this shower and wash away the past two years?"

I smile. "That sounds perfect." I pull her back against me and kiss her with everything I am. I don't want her feeling guilty about what happened to me. Nothing was her fault. She saved me, Jake, and her vaccine saved millions of other people. Without her, I never would have made it through the years of torture that Miles made me endure.

We remove each other's clothes and step into the small, stand-up shower. I spin her around with my lips still on hers. I tilt her head back to let the water flow over her hair while my lips trail down her neck. My lips never leave her skin as my hands massage her head, making sure her hair is soaked.

I stand and pour some shampoo into my hand and begin washing her hair. Our eyes lock and my heart pounds.

"Shouldn't *I* be taking care of *you*? You're the one that lived in hell these past two years."

I shake my head. "Hell is living without you. Now that I have you, I'm never letting go." I tilt her head back and wash the bubbles from her hair. When it's rinsed, she spins me around and starts rubbing me down with the bar of soap. Her touch is so soft it feels foreign to me, but still natural. For the past two years, all I've felt is pain but her touch is something that has never left me. Even when I was being beaten or burned, it was still something I could feel. I would concentrate on the sensation of her fingers grazing my skin, her naked chest flush with mine, or her soft lips showering my body with kisses, and the pain didn't even register anymore.

Before I knew about my son, she was the one thing that got me through.

Once we are both clean I shut off the water and step out of the shower, pulling two towels from the small cabinet. I wrap one around her tightly, and use the other to dry myself off.

"I'll grab you some of Jake's clothes," Brooklyn says, stepping out of the bathroom. She returns a moment later with a pair of pajama pants. "I couldn't see much in there, but I figured this would work for you to sleep in."

"Thank you." I take the pants from her and pull them on. She slides a pair of panties up her long legs and tugs on an over-sized T-shirt, then takes my hand and leads the way down the hall and to the Murphy bed. "Once we are home, in our own bed, there will be no clothes between us."

She softly laughs. "You obviously have no idea what it's like to have a toddler. It won't be just 'our bed' for a while."

We both fall into the bed, and I wrap my arms around her middle, pulling her back to my chest. I listen to her deep breathing, her heartbeat, and let her sweet scent carry me off into a deep, dreamless sleep.

———

I wake in a panic long before the sun rises. Miles is going to know I'm gone soon. I sit upright suddenly, causing Brooklyn to stir awake.

"What's wrong?"

My body is covered in sweat and goosebumps. "We have to get out of here. We have to get to your dad."

"Why? I called him last night and filled him in. He has his top security personnel by him at all times."

"That didn't work out for him so well last time, and Miles is going to know I'm gone soon if he doesn't already. He's going to be looking for me, but not before he hires someone else to take out your dad. We need to get there."

"Can't a guy get some rest around here?" Jake says, sitting up and rubbing his eyes.

"Not today, bro. It's time to run." I stand from the bed and pull Brooklyn up with me. "Go get dressed," I tell her with a swat to her ass. She giggles and walks back to the bathroom.

Once she is no longer in view, I sit on the edge of the bed and look at Jake. "I'm sorry for bringing this all back into your life."

He looks at me like he can't believe what I'm saying. "What the hell are you talking about? We're just happy you're alive. We'll take care of the rest of this shit. Besides, if you didn't need my help, you wouldn't have sent me a text."

"I want you to take Brooklyn back home. I never expected you to bring her with you. I don't want her involved with this shit."

"No fucking way!" Brook is back and she's fuming mad.

"Fuck," falls from my lips.

She marches over to me and kneels in front of me. "I've lost you once, I'm not doing it again. We're going with you."

I meet her dark eyes. "What about John? He needs someone to protect him, someone who knows what's going on and what dangers are really out there."

She shakes her head. "We have a safe room and the nanny knows all about our past. She's not your typical nanny. She's a part of the secret service. She's a trained bodyguard. John will be fine."

I stand and start pacing with my hands on my head. "There's no talking you two out of this, is there?"

"Not a chance," Jake says.

I stop my pacing and look at them both. "Do you even know what we're about to get into?"

Brook nods and Jake shrugs. "Whatever it is, we'll be together," Brooklyn says as she stands and walks closer to me. She takes my hand in hers.

I look at our joined hands and back up to her dark eyes. "Alright. It's time to get out of here."

Everyone springs to action without hesitation. Twenty minutes later, just as the sun starts to peek over the horizon, we are all dressed and ready.

I tuck one of the small pistols from the black bag into the waistband of my jeans. "Let's go. The race is on," I say as I open the door and lead them down the stairs.

I stop at the edge of the building and peek around the corner, scanning the lot before us. "Which car is yours?" I ask them before stepping out into the open.

"The blue Jeep Wrangler that's parked in the front row," Brooklyn replies.

"Alright. Let's go." I step from the side of the building and keep my head down while walking as quickly as possible.

Nothing seems out of the ordinary as Jake gets behind the wheel. I take the passenger seat while Brooklyn gets in the backseat. We toss our bags back to her.

"Where to?" Jake asks.

"DC," I tell him.

He nods before pressing on the clutch and shifting into first gear. He pulls out of the parking spot, turning left to exit the lot. As we pull up to the street, a familiar black Hummer turns slowly into the lot.

My eyes zero in on the men in the front seat. One of them I've never seen before, but the other is Miles. I lean back so he doesn't see my face. "Jake!" I yell loud enough that he looks over at me.

"What the hell?"

"That is Miles pulling into the parking lot. Don't let him see your face, but pull out of here as calmly as possible. We don't want to draw any attention to ourselves."

We both look back at the entrance, but the Hummer has already turned and is parking.

"Go!" I tell him.

Jake pulls out onto the street and drives as casually as possible until we're no longer in their line of sight, then he hits the gas and shifts into sixth gear, blowing through stop signs and traffic lights.

"Why didn't you just take him out?" Brook asks from the backseat.

"You think Miles goes anywhere without protection? He sent his minion into the apartment while he sits in the car, surrounded by bullet proof glass. This is our safest option right now."

"If you smashed the bracelet, how do you think he found you?" Jake asks.

I shrug. "Who knows. Maybe that was the last location it recorded before it was smashed. We're on our own now so let's get this shit done."

Jake turns onto the freeway and heads in the direction of DC. I sit back and pray that this is all over soon. I want my life back. I want my family back. And I want Miles gone forever.

CHAPTER ELEVEN

Brooklyn

"Yes, Dad, we are headed your way. We need to come up with a plan to keep all of us safe. Yes, I know you have men for that, but this has to be stopped one way or another. We can't keep letting Miles ruin our lives and if your men haven't been able to find any dirt on him, then we have to find a way to get some solid evidence against him. He's going to send men after you. Please be extra careful. We'll see you tonight." I don't even put the phone away.

"Hi, Grace. How is J-Man?" John turns and gives me an odd look from the front seat. "Yes, we found him, and we'll be bringing him home as soon as we tie up some loose ends here. Give him a kiss for me." I throw my phone in my purse and dig out a hair tie so I can pull my hair up into a ponytail.

"You call him J-Man?" John finally asks.

"That is my nickname for him and it kind of stuck," Jake answers him, grinning.

"J-Man," John repeats looking down. "I hate that I've missed out on so much with him."

I place my hand on his shoulder. "Hey, you have a lifetime with him now. You're going to be a great dad. Next kiddo though, I want you in the delivery room." I laugh out loud.

"Hey now, once I got up off the floor, I did fine." Jake looks at me in the rearview mirror.

"This I have to hear." John turns in his seat with the most beautiful smile on his face. He never seems to get to be happy for very long, but once I get him home, I plan on keeping him that way. "He passed out cold as soon as the baby came out."

"He was all gooey," Jake says with a look of disgust.

John laughs so hard he snorts. "I can't believe you passed out."

"Just wait, you'll see. Those little suckers are gross when they come out."

I smack Jake in the back of the head. "He was beautiful."

John loses the smile that was covering his face. "At least you got to see him be born."

The Jeep starts sputtering. "Oh, shit."

"Don't tell me we're out of gas?" John says looking at the gauge, tapping it with his finger.

"Okay, I won't tell you then." Jake offers up a nervous grin.

"Look, there's a gas station right there on the left." I point over his shoulder.

We're lucky. It stalls out right in front of the pump. "I'm going to go get some Munchies while you pump the gas." I open the back door and John is on my heels.

"No Funyons for you." He wraps his arm around my waist. "I want to be able to make out with you in the back seat and those things stink." He kisses my temple as we walk into the store.

"I'll forgo them for a make out session with you. Which base do you plan on making it to?" I tease with him.

"I'm always up for a homerun." He swats my ass and heads over to the coffee.

I load up on chips, Pop Tarts, crackers, candy, and finish it off with a supersized Icee before meeting John back at the register. He's wearing a pair of sunglasses with the little plastic tag hanging down in the middle.

"Do you plan on sharing any of that?" He slides the glasses to the edge of his nose.

I lay the items down on the counter and face him. "These are all for me." I reach behind him and grab his ass. Then I steal the sunglasses. "I'm taking these too." I place them on the counter. He leans in and kisses the top of my shoulder.

"I'm going to have to get a second job just to feed you." He sneaks in and grabs a candy bar.

"Hey, get your own!"

He peels off the wrapper and bites off half, then sticks the other half in front of my mouth. "It's called sharing." He laughs at my pouting lip.

I hug my bag to my body and walk past him. Jake is finishing up pumping the fuel. "What did you get me?"

"You're as bad as your brother. These are mine. I think he's inside stocking up for the two of you."

"You've got like two huge bags there. You aren't going to share any of it?"

I open the back door and throw the bags inside. John comes up behind me with a Twizzler hanging out of his mouth. "Here," he hands a bag to Jake, "I'd keep these away from her if I were you." He steals the sunglasses from my face and slides them on, getting in the back seat with me.

We climb in and Jake eases out into traffic. All I can think about is making out with John. I place my hand on his thigh and begin tracing my fingers up and down his leg.

"What are you doing?"

"You said we could make out." I bat my eyes at him.

I yelp when he straddles me over his lap. He bites my lip and then kisses me. I'm breathless when I come up for air, but I notice the car behind us. "Um... isn't that Miles' Hummer?"

He nearly throws me off his lap while turning around to look. "Fuck, how does he keep finding me? Step on it Jake!"

"There is a traffic jam out in front of us," he says.

John leans over the backseat and takes out his gun. "You need to trade places with Jake."

"What? You want me to drive?"

"Yes, I need Jake back here with me fighting them off. Besides, you're a better driver and Jake's a better shot."

Jake starts to slow down. "No, we need to keep going. Make the change before we get to a dead standstill behind that traffic."

"You want us to switch places while we're still moving?" I look at him like he's crazy.

"Yes, and hurry your sweet ass up."

I climb over the seat and sit as close to Jake as I can. "You lean up and I'll go under you." He takes one hand off the wheel and puts it on the door for support. As he leans up, I slide under him, causing him to bump his head on the roof of the Jeep, and we jerk to the right. He manages to gain control just before we run off the road.

"Grab the wheel," he yells. He slides off me, keeping his foot on the gas pedal. "Are you ready?"

"I got it, I got it," I say as my heart races. I watch in the rearview mirror as Jake climbs over the seat, and John hands him a weapon. As we get close to the traffic jam, I increase my speed, and shift into sixth gear, running it off into the shoulder. The Jeep bounces, flinging Jake against the door.

"Shit, Brook!"

"Sorry." I shrug.

"Don't be sorry. Whatever you do, don't stop," John says. He climbs in the very back and smashes the window out with the butt of his gun. Jake hangs partially out the window. "Aim for the tires, his glass is bulletproof!" he yells.

Shots start flying as the Hummer gains on us. Keeping both hands on the wheel, I make it past the traffic jam and weave in and out of lanes, trying to out run them. I swerve in between two semis and Jake is flung over to the other side of the Jeep.

"Jesus Brooklyn, we're trying to kill Miles, not me!" he says, rubbing the top of his head.

"Get back over in the far right lane, there's a bridge coming up!" John yells out. I swerve again, flinging Jake back over to the other side. When he recovers he glares at me the rearview mirror.

"Next time I'm driving," he growls.

The Hummer is right on our bumper. John is hanging half way out the back. "Um...John...you might want to get inside." The road to the bridge is backed up and I have no choice but to take the access road leading down to the retaining wall. Jake pulls John in as the Jeep takes flight, flying downward until we hit the bottom. It only backed them off a little. I swerve the Jeep toward the sloped wall, sending both of them to the left side. I drive up the wall and the Hummer follows. Up ahead I can see where the wall ends abruptly. I speed up and wait until the last minute, pulling the steering wheel to the left directly down toward the water.

Miles' vehicle can't recover in time. It flies off the retaining wall into a fence before landing in the water. "Brooklyn, watch out!" John yells. I turn the vehicle sharply, sending us on two wheels. We barely miss going into the river. Gravity pulls the Jeep back down onto all four tires with a heavy thud.

"I'm so sorry. I was so busy watching what happened to Miles, I forgot to turn." John climbs over the seat and plants a kiss on my cheek.

"You did awesome, baby." Jake is in the back seat hooting and hollering.

"That was amazing!" he yells. He reaches over and kisses the back of my head.

"Don't get too excited," John says, pointing up on the bridge. "There are cops headed our way. Pull over and let me drive."

I stop and he gets out. I slide over into the passenger side and buckle up. He takes off, driving us back up on the main road. Flashing lights are headed in our direction and gaining fast. John weaves in and out between cars across six lanes of traffic, pushing the speedometer up to 120mph. A brief gap appears in traffic and he jerks the wheel, careening our vehicle from the far left lane into the far right lane. The sound of screeching tires fills the air as cars behind us slam on their brakes to avoid collision. Several of them crash into each other, scattering glass and metal across the highway. A semi swerves around us, brakes squealing and smoking, close enough to take off our side mirror. We hit the off-ramp at full speed and struggle to stay in control around the tight radius, but manage to wrestle the car to safety. Several of the vehicles that piled up have formed a smoking barrier in front of the ramp, preventing the cops from following us.

"We're going to need to take another route to keep us off the highway for now. Pull up a map on your phone," he says.

I lay my head on his shoulder. "Do you think we lost him for good?"

"I don't know. He has to know we're headed for DC, but I don't know how he keeps finding us."

I rub my hand across his chest, weaving my hand inside his shirt. I can't keep from touching him. I want to know that he is real. My fingers touch the star-shaped scar on his chest, feeling the lump of the bullet underneath.

"I know how he's doing it." I pick my head up and look at him.

"How?"

"It wasn't the bracelet that was the tracker, it's the bullet. You said it had some type of nanotechnology. That has to be it. We need to get it out of you."

CHAPTER TWELVE

John

"Get off the freeway!" Brook yells.

I swerve over just in time to take the next exit. As soon as the Jeep is in park, I pull my shirt off and examine the puckered scar. I run my fingers across it, applying a little pressure, and I can feel the knot of something inside me. I never thought much of it before, but I think Brook's right. It's the only thing that makes any sense.

We're outside of a small town, surrounded by small farmsteads, grazing livestock, and fields. In front of us, at the end of the main road, is a small grocery store, gas station, and a veterinarian clinic.

"I'll pull in there." I point at the small brick veterinarian's office up the road a ways and put the Jeep back in drive.

I pull into the parking lot and shut off the car. "Now what?" Jake asks as I grab some cash out of my bag.

"Stay here and keep a lookout. Don't let anyone inside." I jump out of the Jeep with Brooklyn on my heels.

"Do you really think they are just going to cut that thing out of you?"

"I bet they will with a gun to their head," I whisper as I swing open the door and allow her to walk in ahead of me.

A sweet looking elderly lady with graying hair is sitting behind the front counter. "Can I help you?" She stands from her chair.

"Yes, I need to see the doctor."

"He's in with a patient right now. Is there something I can do for you?" I watch as her eyes drink me in.

"No, I have a sick dog and was needing to ask some questions."

Just then a man in a white coat walks into the waiting room with a Great Dane and its owner. "I think he'll be just fine as long as we can keep him on a diet," the doctor says, shaking the owner's hand.

I wait for the dog and owner to leave before I turn to the doctor. "Excuse me, sir. Would you mind giving me a minute of your time?"

He turns to face me, confusion written on his face. He looks at my shirtless chest and answers, "Sure, what can I do for you?" His voice is brimming with questions, but he manages to be patient with me.

I look around at the lady behind the desk. "Can we speak in private?"

The older man shrugs and leads me down a hallway and into his office.

"What can I do for you, young man?" He sits down behind his desk.

I take the seat across from him and point at the star-shaped scar. "There is something inside of me, and I need you to get it out."

The man throws his head back laughing. "Son, I can assure you, there is nothing inside of you. And even if there were, I'm a vet. I work on animals, not humans."

I lean in. "Well, here's the thing. I was shot two years ago with a bullet that surrounds a tracking device. I need it taken out. That's not something you can go to the hospital for."

The old man scoffs. "No such technology even exists. I suggest you get off the marijuana, son." He stands and moves to open the door.

I stand quickly and pull the gun out of the back of my waistband. "Humor me."

He freezes mid-step and holds his hands up. "Do you even know how to use that weapon you're holding in your hand?"

"I know more than you would think," I say without moving.

He runs his hand through his white hair. "Alright. Let's go to an exam room."

I motion with the gun for him to walk. He opens the door and turns down the hallway. I look back at Brooklyn in the waiting room. She's leaning over the counter, talking to the older lady, trying to keep her busy so she doesn't stumble upon something she can't un-see.

"Have a seat on the table," he tells me as he moves around the room, gathering things he needs.

I sit on the cold metal table and watch as he wheels over a cart and uncovers the instruments.

"Normally, I'd like to do an x-ray, but I feel like we don't have the time for that."

"You're right there. I need this out as fast as possible before whoever is tracking me down finds me again."

"This is just a local anesthetic." He picks up a needle and injects the clear solution near the scar. "Are you in some sort of trouble, son?"

"You can say that. I have some very bad people after me and my family."

He puts the syringe down and rubs his fingers over the scar. I see his expression change from annoyed to intrigued. "I think you're right. I can feel something under your skin. How long has it been here?"

"Two years," I answer.

He shakes his head and lets out a whistle. "Two years? It's going to be wrapped up in scar tissue. That anesthetic I gave you may not cover it. I may need to put you out."

"No way. I can handle the pain, trust me."

He shrugs. "It's up to you. Are you ready?"

I nod.

He places the scalpel against my skin and slices in a downward motion. I feel nothing but the warm blood that is running over my chest and soaking into the band of my jeans. He grabs the tweezers and sticks them in the hole in my chest.

His eyes go wide and his eyebrows raise when he gets ahold of the bullet.

"I can feel it. But it's wrapped up in tissue. I'll have to cut it out."

"Do what you have to do, Doc."

"Lie back," he tells me while picking up another instrument which I have never seen before.

I lie back and look up at the lights. Before I know it, I'm hit with a blinding pain and the smell of my flesh burning. I grab the edges of the table while stifling back a scream.

"Almost got it," he says, grabbing the tweezers.

The shot he gave me does nothing. I can feel him digging around inside my chest while the stench of my skin burning washes over me. A second later, I hear the clank of the bullet hitting the table.

"Almost done now. I just have to finish cauterizing and stitch you up. How about since you're here already, you let me take a look at that hand of yours? It looks pretty swollen."

"Thanks, but no thanks. I've spent too much time here already."

Within twenty minutes of walking in the door, the bullet is out and I'm cleaned up. He hands me the bullet, wrapped tightly in gauze. I take it out and inspect the blood-stained bullet. It's the same one that was missing from the case I found.

I hold out my hand to shake. "Thank you. I'm sorry for aiming the gun at you, I just really needed this thing out of me."

He nods. "Please leave and take that thing with you."

I laugh. "I will. You'll never see me again," I promise him.

I walk back out into the waiting room and find Brooklyn petting a cat that's sitting on the counter. "Are you ready?" she asks.

"Yes, let's go."

We both walk out to the Jeep and climb inside. "Did he get it out?" Jake asks as he starts the Jeep.

I pull the gauze from my pocket and show them the bullet.

"Why are you still carrying it around? They're still tracking us." Jake's voice is laced with concern.

"I couldn't leave it there," I tell him. "He would have had that poor old man killed for helping me. I'll get rid of it soon."

Within an hour, we're on a bridge that stretches over a creek. I roll my window down and throw it as hard as I can into the water, hoping it gets carried off in the opposite direction of where we're going.

———

WE'VE BEEN IN THE CAR FOR SEVERAL HOURS NOW, and sitting in this position for so long has my chest sore. Anytime I pick up my arm to turn up the radio, reach for my drink, or just try to turn and look at Brooklyn, a pain shoots through my chest.

Finally, Brook sits up. "Here, take one of these."

I take the bottle from her hand and study it. "What is this?"

"It's pain medication. I stole it from the clinic while you were back getting that bullet removed. I figured you would need it and knew that he wouldn't give it to you since it's technically for animals."

I read over the bottle. One pill per every twenty pounds. I try and count in my head how many I will need to take, but the pain is getting to be unbearable. I give up on my pathetic math skills and pour out fifteen tiny pills. They are small, round pills that are brown in color.

"They're even beef-flavored," Brooklyn says from the backseat. I can hear the amusement in her voice.

"I do love a good steak," I say before throwing them into my mouth and chasing it with a drink of water.

They both look at my scrunched-up nose. "That does not taste like beef." They both laugh while I reach under my seat and pull out the bottle of bourbon I picked up from the gas station. I unscrew the cap and pour some into my mouth, gargling with it in hopes of getting the taste of the pills out of my mouth.

"Do you really think it's a good idea to chase pain killers with alcohol?" Brooklyn asks.

I shake the bottle at her. "They're not that strong. They are for little bitty dogs." I roll my eyes.

"Let me see that." She motions for the bottle. I hand it over and she reads over the label. "How many of these did you take?"

"Fifteen," I answer.

"John, do you realize you should have taken nine? Ten at the most?"

I look over to see Jake staring at me, wide eyed.

"I'm sorry! I can't think straight when I'm in this much pain." I rub the lines that are forming on my forehead as I lean back, trying to get comfortable.

Brooklyn smacks me across the back of the head. "You're such an idiot. Why didn't you ask me how many to take?"

I glance back at her. "Why didn't you tell me how many to take?"

"Alright, guys. It'll be okay," Jake interrupts. "We'll just have to keep an eye on him, that's all."

Brooklyn crosses her arms over her chest and leans back. I turn and face the front. My chest feels like someone reached into it and squeezed everything inside.

Jake looks at us both before saying, "How about we stop and get some food? You probably need something in your stomach with all that pain medication."

"That sounds perfect. I'm starving," Brooklyn perks up from the backseat.

I grow more and more tired as we drive towards town, undoubtedly due to the pain pills taking effect but the moment I sit down in the chair at the restaurant, everything kicks in full force.

My head spins and my blood feels like it's pumping faster. Every light I look at has a bright haze around it. My vision blurs behind my heavy eyelids, but I'm in a great mood. Everything is beautiful and happy.

I feel someone watching me. I look over to see my brother squinting and flexing his jaw.

"Hi, Jake! It's good seeing you. Where have you been?" I ask.

He looks at a drop-dead-sexy redhead and back at me. "What are you talking about? I've been with you the whole time."

"'What am I talking about?' What are *you* talking about? I haven't seen you since you left for college. Who's this?" I nod toward the beautiful girl. "Is she your girlfriend, the sexy little freshmen that you were talking about schooling in love making?" I laugh.

The girl rubs her temples as I lean forward. "What's your name?"

She smiles as her eyes flash back and forth between Jake and I. "Brooklyn."

"That's such a pretty name. I'm Mark." I hold my hand across the table to shake.

She laughs and shakes her head. "No, you're John."

"Wow, that does sound familiar. But who's Mark?"

Jake places his hand on my shoulder and I turn to look at him.

"Are you okay, buddy?"

Suddenly, I've forgotten what we were even talking about. "Yeah, I just have to take a piss," I say, pushing my chair back.

"Shh, stop yelling," the redhead says.

I look around and every eye is on me. I grin. "They think I'm sexy, that's why they're staring."

She shakes her head as Jake slaps me on the back. "Come on, buddy. I'll walk you to the bathroom. We need to wash our hands before we eat anyway."

"Alright." I stand, feeling a little dizzy. Thankfully, Jake keeps his arm around my shoulders, leading me away.

We walk past the buffet and something catches my eye. It's a chocolate fountain. The brown liquid is pouring over the edges, and it looks delicious. I have to taste it. I shrug free from Jake's arm and run toward the chocolate, never taking my eyes off it. I lean down and stick my tongue under the flowing chocolate, lapping it up. It's thick, and warm and creamy, better tasting than I could have imagined.

"Excuse me, sir. You can't do that." I'm pushed away from the flowing goodness. I try wiping the chocolate from my chin.

Jake is back at my side. "I'm sorry, he's a little under the weather, if you know what I mean. I'll pay for the entire fountain."

I stop paying attention to their boring conversation and turn back to the buffet. It's lined with delicious food. Who just leaves all this food lying here? I grab the big spoon that's in the mashed potatoes and take a big bite. It's hot and thick.

I open my mouth and let the burning potatoes fall off my tongue and back into the container. The chocolate I just ate is covering the fluffy, white potatoes like a thick gravy. I shake off the disgust, grabbing a piece of chicken off the bar. I take a bite and walk around eating it while looking over the other selections. When my eyes land on freshly-cut steak, I throw the drumstick over my shoulder and make my way toward the perfectly grilled piece of meat. It's glistening from the overhead lights, calling my name.

Just as I'm about to reach out and take it from the lady holding the plate, I'm pulled back. "Time to go," Jake says, tugging me toward the door.

"Wait, I'm hungry!" I yell as I try turning back for the food. I see the redhead get up and chase after us.

"Jake, I'm totally going to bang your girlfriend."

"She's not my girlfriend, you idiot. She's yours."

I turn around, no longer worried about the food. "She's mine?" I laugh. "I'm totally going to bang her then."

Jake shoves me into the car and takes his place behind the wheel. "Five-hundred dollars!" He looks at me in anger.

"What? For what?" I ask. I hear the girl in the back-seat giggle. I turn and flash her a grin.

"For what? Because you tainted their entire buffet! They have to remake all that food!"

"What? I didn't ruin their food." I wave my hand through the air to blow him off.

He starts the Jeep and turns to look at me again. His eyes are angry and he has a little wrinkle between them. "You stuck your tongue under the chocolate fountain, you spit in the mashed potatoes, and you threw a piece of chicken over your shoulder and it hit an old lady!"

I laugh before turning back to the girl in the backseat. She's laughing quietly to herself. "You're mine?" I ask her.

She laughs and nods.

"Thank God! I thought I was going to have to bang my brother's girlfriend." I crawl into the backseat, kicking Jake as I do so. I feel the vehicle swerve before it's righted again.

"Watch it!" he yells at me.

I get into the backseat and turn toward the girl. "You're fucking hot!" I tell her before leaning in for kiss.

Her lips move with mine and she tastes amazing.

I'm nowhere near done when she gently pushes me away. "I think you need to get some rest."

"Why? I feel fine. I do have to piss though, and I'm hungry. Can we stop for food?"

"No!" They both shout at the same time.

I cross my arms over my chest and sit back. A pain forms in my chest and I lift my shirt up to inspect it. "What's this?" I try to remove the bandage.

"Leave that alone!" the girl yells as she pushes my hands away from the bandage. I let my hands fall onto my lap and she pulls my shirt back down.

"What happened to me? Did I have surgery?"

"Well, sort of. You had to get a bullet removed," she tells me.

"A bullet? Like I was shot?"

She nods.

"That's fucking awesome. I was shot with a real bullet? I must be a superhero! How many people get shot in the heart and live?"

She laughs and shakes her head. "You weren't shot in the heart, but you are my superhero. Lay back and just relax."

Her fingers run through my hair, instantly relaxing me. I feel my lids getting heavy as they fight to stay open. Before I know it, I'm out completely.

CHAPTER THIRTEEN

John

*M*y head hurts and my mouth is so dry I could spit dirt. I don't even have the strength to open my eyes yet. I've slept so well. I curl to the right and my nostrils fill with a terrible smell. I peek one eye open and see a pair of ugly feet inches from my nose. "What the hell?" I roll the other direction. After I rub my scruffy face, I lay my hand on my chest. That's when I feel the dressing on it.

Oh, yeah. I remember having the bullet removed and getting back in the car, but where the hell am I now? I lift my head off the pillow to look up. Brooklyn is laying halfway on the bed to the left and Jake's head is at the foot of the bed. His mouth is hanging open and he's drooling all over the sheets. How the hell did I end up in the middle of whatever this is? I'm bare chested. I pull the covers up that are sandwiched underneath me. *At least I still have my jeans on.*

Brooklyn has a long t-shirt on, but it's hiked up showing her red lacey panties. Jake is lying on his stomach in a pair of boxers that have little yellow Minions all over them. No wonder the man never gets laid. I reach down and softly touch Brooklyn's inner thigh. She squirms a little and then curls into a ball with her head laying on my legs.

I don't recall getting a motel room. And why the hell is there only one bed? "Brook," I whisper while shaking my leg. She jumps out of bed with her fists in the air.

"What?! Where is he?" She turns, looking around the room.

I can't help but laugh at her reaction. "You're okay. There's nobody here but us." I raise my right arm and rest my hand behind my head. "Thanks for wanting to save me though."

She tugs her shirt down and smooths her red locks into place, then kneels by the side of the bed. "How are you feeling?"

"I have a feeling, better than I deserve. What happened after we left the vet's office?"

"You don't remember?" She laughs, causing Jake to stir and move closer to me.

"I recollect you giving me some nasty, beef-flavored pills for pain. After that, I'm drawing a blank."

"Oh my God, it was so funny. Except that you ruined dinner and I'm still hungry." She laughs harder.

Jake's foot lands on my face. "Hey, man!" I shove him and he rolls over. His boner is tenting his boxers, sticking into my leg. I throw the covers off and jump out of bed. "Jake! What the hell!" I point at it. "You touched me with your Minion!" Brooklyn is on the floor roaring in laughter.

He hops up and pulls the sheet over him. "It's morning, man," he says tugging it tightly around his waist. His face turns red before he walks off, slamming the bathroom door behind him.

Brooklyn is snorting. "It's not funny! That thing was touching me." My hands are on my hips as I shiver with disgust.

She tries to quit laughing as she uses the bed to climb off the floor. "Oh, where is your sense of humor?" Her lips land on mine, but she continues to laugh.

"Can you please tell me how we ended up in a motel with only one bed?" I try to keep a straight face, but I can't help cracking a smile at her. She's so beautiful in the morning. My hands skate under her t-shirt to cop a quick feel.

"Keep that up and Jake won't be the only one standing out here with a hard-on." She pokes me in the stomach.

I reach between us and adjust myself. "At least it will be touching you."

"Poor Jake. Don't pick on him."

"Pick on him? I've been held captive, chased, had a vet remove a bullet, and... somewhere in there I remember a river of chocolate." I smack my lips together trying to recall when I had chocolate. "And where do potatoes come into the picture?"

She giggles. "Yes, poor Jake. He has to put up with you. At least you have me." She plants a kiss on my nose. "Do you recall anything about wanting to get it on with Jake's girlfriend?" She steps back in full-out laughter again.

My brows furrow. "Jake doesn't have a girlfriend? Besides, I wouldn't want or need anyone but you. How could you say such a thing?" Now, I'm offended.

Jake comes bounding out of the bathroom, tucking his shirt in his jeans. "Yeah, what about trying to have sex with my girl?" He puts his arm around Brook's shoulder. "And, you owe me five hundred dollars."

"I think the two of you have been smoking something funny." I storm off into the bathroom and turn on the hot shower. I look into the mirror at my scruffy face. I wish I could shave. I peel off the dressing from my chest. The wound is red and angry looking. "Great, all I need is a bigger scar." I throw my jeans on the floor and get in the shower. The hot water feels incredible running down my aching body. A breeze of cool air rushes in as the curtain draws back. A pair of hands snake around my waist.

"I hope to God, this isn't Jake." I feel Brook's smile against my back. "Well, if it was, you'd have a boner sticking between your butt cheeks right now."

I straighten up and turn in her arms. "That is not even funny." I pull her into the stream of water with me. She pulls back, laughing and spewing water. "I'd rather have these pressed against me." I pull her closer and kiss the swell of her breast.

"You really don't remember last night?"

"No. And, with you in my arms right now, I really don't care." I push her against the wall and when her lips part with a gasp, my tongue finds its way inside her sweet mouth. My need for her is overwhelming and grows stronger every day. Not just sexually - I need her in every way imaginable. She hikes her leg over my hip and I push my fingers inside her, pene-trating her warmth. She lets out a loud, arousing moan.

"Please." she says, breathless.

I take her hands and pin them against the shower wall. "Please what?" I bite at the spot just below her ear. My teeth graze the sensitive skin and her moans grow louder, sexier, more provocative.

"I want you buried deep inside me."

I yank her leg higher and thrust deep inside her. She lets out a scream. "Deep enough for you, baby?" I ask.

Her lust-filled eyes lock on mine. "No, deeper."

"Fuck me," I groan, shifting my weight to one side. I bend one knee slightly and thrust my hips upward.

"Yes!" she screams.

I thrust and stop, thrust and stop. In between, I roll her nipple in my mouth. She breaks my grip from her wrists and pulls my hair hard, tugging my head backward. "Don't stop." Her words are my breaking point. I find the perfect spot that makes her moans grow raw and needier for me. I don't stop until she's screaming my name and I've let go with her.

We both come down kissing one another. I kiss her neck. She kisses my chest. Our hands are lingering on each other's bodies. I can't get enough of this woman. Every time I have her, I want her even more. Our moment is broken by a knock on the door.

"Guys, it's getting a little uncomfortable out here. Not only can I hear you, even with plugging my ears, but I'm sure the entire motel can hear you."

We both start laughing. I kiss her one last time. "We really should get back on the road."

We wash each other, then towel each other off. I pull my jeans back on and rummage through Jake's bag to find a shirt. Brooklyn shimmies into a pink thong and pulls on a pair of skinny jeans with a white flowing shirt.

Jake is standing in front of the window, peeking out the curtain. "Did someone follow us?" I ask as I pull on my black boots.

"No, there is no sign of Miles." He turns around to face us. "If there are no more mishaps, we should be in DC around dinner time. You might want to call your dad and let him know. Are we going to the White House?"

"No. We're going to meet him at my apartment." Brook says, running a brush through her mop of hair.

"You kept it?" I ask.

"Yeah. I figured if I ever went back, I'd have a place for J-Man and I to stay. I hate going into the White House."

I pick up our bags from the floor. "Do you still have the bullet I stole from Miles?" I place my hand out, palm side up.

"Yeah," she digs around in her purse and places the bullet in my hand.

"Do you plan on killing Miles with that?" Jake asks, opening the motel room door.

"I'll either kill him or track him with it," I answer, following him down the stairs.

"I vote we take him out permanently," Brooklyn says, skipping down behind us.

Jake climbs in behind the driver's seat. "I call shotgun," Brooklyn squeals, and runs to the other side. I throw our gear through the broken window in the back and get in the back seat, sitting in the middle.

"Keep your eyes peeled for anyone following us. We don't want to lead anyone to your father. Give him a call and tell him to be vigilant. Miles may have already sent someone to do the job for him."

She puts on her sunglasses and gets her phone out. He answers on the first ring, and she tells him our plan. She puts him on speaker phone.

"I've lined up extra men for protection. I'll send a few of them over to your apartment to make sure the coast is clear. I'll have two FBI cars in front of me and two behind me on the way to your apartment. I'll be perfectly safe," he says.

"Okay, Dad."

"Love you, Brooky. Oh, and John?"

"Yes, sir?" I sit taller when he's talking directly to me.

"I'm glad you're alive."

"Thank you, sir."

We finish the drive to DC and park in front of the apartment. Dad wasn't kidding, it seems the whole block is surrounded in security vehicles. Nobody would be stupid enough to try something with this many guards here.

We all climb out of the Jeep and make our way to the front doors. I have to show my I.D. to a guard just to get into my own apartment building. Another guard, posted outside the elevator, nods at us in acknowledgement and pushes the button for the elevator.

I mumble a polite thank you and stand, waiting. When the doors open, the guard thoroughly searches the inside for us, even lifting the crawl space in the ceiling to make sure nobody is waiting for us. When he has it secured, he nods us on and says, "There will be another guard on your floor as well."

The three of us step into the elevator and Jake pushes the button for my floor. "Damn, your dad is getting serious."

I let out a laugh. "About time. I swear that man has a Superman complex. He acts like he's made of steel."

Within seconds, the elevator opens and we step out to see another guard standing by the elevator on this floor. "The president has been informed that you have arrived, Ms. Warren."

"Thank you, Jeeves," I joke as I pass by, leading the way.

Jake bumps my shoulder with his. "Is his name really Jeeves?"

I laugh and shake my head. "How should I know?"

A guard is outside my apartment, and he opens the door, allowing us to walk in. My dad is pacing across the floor when we walk in, with his head down and hands laced behind his back. He turns around and smiles when he hears us, holding his arms out at his sides for a hug.

I rush into them. "I'm so glad you're okay." He wraps his arms around me and kisses the top of my head.

When he releases me, he holds out his hand to John. "I'm glad to see that you're okay."

John shakes his hand. "Thank you, sir. I wish this meeting was under better circumstances, but unfortunately, if I'm involved, it's usually not good," he jokes.

"You haven't changed a bit, have you?" My dad laughs.

He turns to Jake and shakes his hand. "Jake, good to see you again. How's that stock doing that I gave you advice on?"

He smiles. "It's doing great. I've already more than tripled my money and it continues to go up every day."

John smacks him on the back of his head. "And you were hassling me over five-hundred bucks?"

Jake shrugs. "I've worked hard for that money."

"Alright, guys. You all seem to bicker as much as you always did. Let's get down to business, huh?"

The guys settle down on the sofa and chairs that surround the coffee table in the center while I grab a few beers from the fridge. I hand them each one and sit down, pulling out my phone.

"Who could you possibly be calling right now?" my dad asks me.

"I'm ordering in. I haven't eaten in forever. Someone got us kicked out of a restaurant last night." I look directly at John.

His brows raise in surprise. "Okay, someone is going to have to tell me what the fuck went on last night!"

"Put your phone away. I'll send one of the guys out for something. God knows you're not picky," Dad says, rolling his eyes.

I set the phone down in front of me and take a drink of my beer while my dad dictates orders to his men. As soon as someone is on the way to get us food, my dad adjusts his jacket and looks at John. "Okay, tell me what all is going on."

John starts his story from the beginning, telling my dad everything from the time we thought he was dead up to this very moment. My dad sits back, taking in all the information.

Before anyone can speak again, the door opens and a guard enters, arms full of bags. I stand and chase him to the kitchen, eager to see everything he picked up.

I grab a plate and load it down with pizza, pasta, and breadsticks. I place my overflowing plate on the coffee table and the three guys look at me, still amazed that I eat as much as I do. Jake leans forward, reaching his hand out for a breadstick, but I slap it down. "Go get your own!"

"Geez, alright Stingy."

My dad looks completely stressed. His jacket is now off, lying over the back of his chair, and his tie has been loosened. "Why don't we have some dinner before trying to figure all this out." He stands and slowly walks into the kitchen.

I look at John. "Do you think he's going to be alright? He looks a little stressed."

John stands and moves down to the end of the couch to be closer to me. "He's a tough man. We'll figure all this out so we can move on and live normal lives."

I grin up at him. "Normal, kinky lives?"

He lets out a roar of laughter. "I wouldn't have it any other way with you."

I pick up a slice of taco pizza and bring it to my mouth, but he leans forward at the last second and snatches a huge bite. I frown at him. "You're lucky I love you. Nobody comes between me and my taco pizza."

He gives me a playful smile before standing to go make his plate.

———

As the night wears on, the guys run through a long list of ideas about how to stop Miles, but each one is picked apart and thrown away. The clock is about to strike midnight, but we're still no closer to finding an answer.

My dad doesn't want to do anything that could be considered illegal, and John is convinced that whatever happens, he has to be a part of it. He wants to be the one to end his life, and I understand that, but I don't want him going up against Miles again. I want the three of us to go get J-Man and disappear for the rest of our lives while someone else takes care of Miles. I don't want him back in the line of fire.

We all decide to call it a night. Dad takes the spare bedroom, John and I take my room, and Jake is stuck on the couch. All the security men have been replaced with a new set, so they can be alert and awake all night.

We lock up the apartment and retire to our rooms. I strip my clothes off as I cross the room, throwing myself back on the bed in nothing but my panties.

"Ahh, now I remember why I liked this apartment so much. This bed is amazing."

John is walking closer to me, slowly pulling off clothes. His eyes darken as he takes me in. "I have to admit, it does look like a nice bed."

Down to his boxers, he slowly begins to crawl up the bed, planting kisses up my legs, stomach, breasts, and finally on my lips. I wrap my legs around his hips and feel him grow hard against me.

"God, I've missed your touch," I say against his lips.

He tangles his fingers into my hair and yanks my head back so my throat is exposed. He scrapes his teeth along the sensitive skin and my body breaks out with goosebumps. "You don't even know how fucking bad I missed you." His hands travel to my hips while he sits back on his knees, between my legs. His eyes slowly and deliberately take in every inch of me before he pulls the thin material down my thighs. "Not one minute went by that I wasn't thinking about you, hoping you were happy and safe. I would have gladly died to keep you out of harm's way." His finger finds my entrance and he dips inside, spreading my wetness.

"I've longed for the taste of you." His hands move to my ass, squeezing as he lowers his mouth to me. The slow circular motions of his tongue send me spiraling, I grasp the bedsheet and ride out my release on his tongue.

He pulls away and his eyes have only gotten darker. "It was like I could still feel the soft skin of your thighs on my face." He pushes his boxers down. "I could still feel how hot and wet you were when I'd slide into you." He takes himself in his hand and pumps once before positioning himself at my entrance. "I could hear that sound you make when I'm completely filling you with every inch." He pushes forward, holding me by the hips. I gasp as I fist the sheets again.

He finally leans over me while keeping pace. "Shhh, we don't want our guests to hear you screaming my name too many times," he teases.

I dig my nails into his back and roll us over. I look down at him with a smirk. "The only thing they're going to hear is you begging me to stop," I say before lifting myself up and sliding back down his length.

His eyes roll back and close before his hands squeeze my hips. His lips part as a soft moan leaves them. I continue with the motion until he sits up, sucking my hard nipple into his hot mouth. His tongue flicks against it over and over until I'm panting and shattering into a million pieces.

He lifts me off of him, and positions me on my knees. He takes his place behind me and pushes forward. With the position change, he feels even bigger, like he's going even deeper. His hands travel from my breasts to my ass where he squeezes harder with each thrust. Our heavy breathing fills the room as sweat beads up on my skin and rolls off. Just as I shatter again, he lets out a loud moan and fills me with a jerk.

When he collapses at my side, I roll into him, resting my head on his scarred chest. I can hear his heart pounding for me.

I look up at him, placing my hand on his cheek. "I love you, John."

"I love you, Brook," he whispers before pulling me flush against him.

I let my eyes drift closed and feel him press a kiss to my forehead. I drift off to sleep listening to his heart pound, something I thought I'd never experience again.

CHAPTER FIFTEEN

John

I open my eyes to find myself secluded in darkness. I try to stand, but my wrists are tied to a chair. I pull hard against my restraints. It doesn't break. It only digs the rope tighter into my skin. It makes popping and cracking noises from the force, but it doesn't give.

The sound of the heavy metal door scraping across the concrete floor breaks the silence, flooding my cell with a low light.

"Time to play, John. Aren't you excited to see what games we play this time?" the guard asks.

I pull against the ropes again, not bothering to give him any of my attention.

I smell smoke and look up to see the bright orange glow of the end of the cigar he's smoking. I know what game we're playing. I pull harder, I need to get free.

He rushes over to me and sticks the hot end of the cigar to my chest. "Stop fighting and just give in already!" he screams as the cigar scorches my flesh. The smell is harsh and overbearing as it makes it way up my nose. The pain is excruciating. I squeeze my hands into tight fists while grinding my teeth together, trying to hold back the scream that desperately wants to escape me.

He tosses the cigar onto the dirty concrete floor as he takes a step away from me. A wicked smile covers his face as he reaches into his back pocket. My heart pounds as my breathing picks up. What is he going to do this time? There was a time when I thought these sessions couldn't get any worse, but I was wrong. They are getting tired of not being able to break me lately and they are done playing. Each time I'm brought down here, it only gets worse.

He pulls out a pair of plyers as he walks closer. He kneels at my side and grabs my hand. I try keeping my hands balled up, but he pries the left one open, taking my middle finger in between his. He raises the plyers to my finger and pinches the nail.

"One more chance, John. What's is going to be?"

"Fuck you," leaves my lips before I force my eyes closed and wait for the pain to hit me.

I wake with a jerk and check my surroundings. I'm in Brooklyn's apartment. I rub my eyes, hoping to shake off the remnants of the dream. I didn't realize I had fallen asleep.

I laid quietly beside Brooklyn most of the night while she slept. My mind had been racing with potential ways to stop Miles once and for all, not allowing me any rest. I have a feeling he'll be close by. Knox is paying him highly for this job, and he doesn't want it fucked up. He lost his ace when I turned on him. He thought for sure that threatening my family would be the ticket he needed, but he forgot one thing: I consider President Warren my family too. There was no way in Hell I would have killed him. I would have turned the gun on myself first.

The sun is barely starting to peek through the bottom slat in the blinds. I smell coffee and hear soft, deep voices coming from the living room. I gently slide my arm from under Brook's head, shifting until I'm free of her gorgeous body. I'm tempted to curl back into her and slide my hands between her legs, but she needs the rest. Instead, I pull on my jeans and t-shirt.

Her father is sitting on the lounge chair sipping coffee with his legs outstretched on the table. Jake is still sound asleep on the couch. One agent is standing by the window looking out and another stands stoically by the front door. He hears me and turns in my direction. "Good morning. Coffee's made." He lifts his mug in the air.

"Thank you. I could smell it in the bedroom. Did you sleep, sir?" I open up several cabinets looking for a mug. I pour a cup, and join him on the couch.

"Do you play golf?" he asks, blowing on his hot coffee.

"Um, no, I've never really had time for that." What I actually mean is that I've been too busy playing other games with people's lives and that I've screwed mine up, but I don't think that's what he wants to hear.

"I play every Friday morning at an exclusive club."

What's he getting at? I've lost track of my days. Today is... Friday. I put my mug down and turn in his direction. "Today is Friday, sir. I'm sure you already knew that, but I don't think it's a good idea."

"I'll be perfectly safe with all these men around me. I think better, clearer when I'm playing. Why don't you come with me?"

"We've already established the fact that I don't play golf, but besides that, we really need to come up with a plan to keep Miles' men from killing you."

He puts his coffee down. "You and I have had no real time to bond. You've been on the run since the day I met you. I know my daughter loves you, but I'd really like to get the chance to know the father of my grandson. I've always trusted her judgement, but she's either been hunted or hurting from the first day you walked into her life."

I start to say something, but he shuts me down.

"I know that Brooklyn being hunted was not your fault, nor her thinking you were dead." He puts his hand on my shoulder. "I want to know, after all this is said and done, what are you going to do to make my daughter and grandson happy and safe from here on out?"

"I..."

"Don't tell me now." He stands. "Tell me on the golf course."

"Sir, Brooklyn will have my balls if I let you out of her sight."

"Then I suggest we go before she wakes up." He heads for the door and the agent follows him.

"My shoes are in the bedroom." I start in that direction.

"We'll get you some shoes at the club. I don't want to risk your balls." He laughs, opening the door.

———

His agents surround us as we walk to his black limo. As I stare at my bare feet, the absurdity of the situation hits me: I am sitting here in a classy limo next to the President of the United States and I have no shoes on.

He chuckles beside me. "Feeling a little under-dressed?" he says, pointing at my feet.

"Something like that. Sir, are you sure this is a good idea?"

"Getting to know you a little better? Yes. Us leaving without telling Brooky? No way." He pushes number two on his phone. It strikes me as funny that of all the people in the world the President knows and has to deal with, Brooklyn is his first person on speed dial.

Her voice screeches through the phone the moment she answers. He holds the phone at arm's length until he can get a word in edgewise. "If you will stop yelling, I'll explain." More screaming vibrates the phone. "I know, we should have woken you up, but the agents knew where we were going. I left a few there with you and we have an entourage of agents with us. John's never played golf and I want to teach him."

More screaming.

"Yes, I know we should be making a plan. We'll do that when we get back from playing golf. We're going through a tunnel and I'm going to lose you," he says, disconnecting.

I look at the window in front of us and see nothing but traffic. "Sir, there is no tunnel."

"I know that, but she doesn't." He smiles.

———

THE CLUB IS SECLUDED FROM THE CITY. THE VALET attendant opens our door. They obviously know the vehicle and look completely confused when I climb out of the back seat with my bare feet.

"Sir, this is a private club," he says with a deep crease in his brow.

"He's with me," the President says, stepping out of the limo.

"Sorry, sir," he says, ushering us and the agents to the revolving glass doors.

The front desk clerk smiles and nods when she sees him. We bypass the formal entrance and are directed into a private locker room. "He'll need some clothes and shoes," he tells the attendant." He looks me up and down, sizing me up, and disappears.

Matthew punches numbers into a box on his locker and the door pops open. He starts undressing as the attendant comes back in with a light blue pair of cotton pants, a white pullover, and golf shoes that have some sort of tassel on them.

"I think I'll just take the shoes, if that's okay with you?" The attendant looks at me and then at Matthew for approval.

He laughs. "Suit yourself." He throws me a pair of socks from his locker.

I sit down on the bench and put them on along with the stuffy shoes. I stand and rock back and forth, trying to make them more comfortable.

"They take some getting used to," he says while he finishes lacing his well-worn shoes. "Let's go get you some clubs." One of the agents grabs his clubs from another locker and we head out the back door into a lush, green course. A golf cart is already waiting on us. Three, in fact - one for us, and two for the many agents that will be following us.

As we drive down to the first hole, I scan the area. There is no fence surrounding the property. On the south side, lakes cover almost every inch of the perimeter. To the north are lines of trees. I can't help but wonder how secure the property is, but I decide to try and relax a little and learn something new. Who knows - when I get to Maui, maybe I'll take up golfing. For the first time in years, I won't have anyone chasing me and I sure as Hell won't be taking any more contracts. That part of my life is behind me now. I'll make Brooklyn my wife and I'll finally get to meet my son. For the first time ever, my life is looking pretty damn good.

Matthew talks me through everything, including how to swing a club. Every now and then he asks me something personal, but nothing too tough. By the eighth hole, I'm finally relaxed and enjoying myself. It seems that I have a natural ability for golf. I've done pretty well for a first-timer.

The agents are huddled together, kicked back watching us play. Matthew tees up the ball. I shield my eyes from the sun and look down the fairway at the greens.

"I'm really glad we did this," he says, taking a practice swing. "What are you going to do with yourself when this is all over?" He leans on his driver.

"Retire," I chuckle.

"What I really want to know is what are you going to do with my daughter?" He takes a few steps toward me. "She's been through a hell of a lot, you know."

"I plan on spending the rest of my life making her happy. If it's okay with you, I'd like to make her my wife?" I watch his facial expressions for any indication of what he's thinking, but he doesn't show any. I swallow hard and walk closer to him. "I love her, sir, more than the air I breathe. I think I've proven that I will do anything to keep her and our son safe. Things that you may have to pardon me for later. She is the only woman that I have ever loved or will love. I'm nothing without her."

He stares at me for a moment, then sticks out his hand. I place mine in his. "Then you have my blessing. But know this: if anything happens to her or my grandson because of you, there will be no place you can hide that I won't find you."

"I promise to take care of both of them, sir," I say wholeheartedly.

"Then we're good here." He picks up his driver and walks back over to the tee, taking a few more practice swings. A flash from the line of trees reflects off the tip of his club. Instinctively, I dive forward, knocking him to the ground and shielding him with my body. I am too late though, the bullet has already made contact with him. The agents already have their guns drawn, scrambling to provide cover for the president. Blood stains his left shoulder. I pull back his shirt to see how bad it is.

"It's a flesh wound, sir." I stand, taking his hand, helping him up as the agents cluster inches away from us. "Get him inside. I'm going after the shooter." He grabs my arm to stop as I turn in the direction of the shooter.

"Let my men handle it."

"With all due respect, sir, I know these men and I know how they operate. I will handle this, but I need a gun." He instructs one of his agents to give me their gun. I take it and run in a zigzag pattern in the direction that I saw the flash of light. When I make it to the tree line, I look back to see that Matthew and the agents are safely inside.

I aim my gun into the trees. "I know you're up there!" I yell. A bullet sends bark flying from the tree next to me, giving me a direction to go on. I move behind the cover of the tall trees in the direction the bullet came from. Looking through the scope of my rifle, I can distinguish a boot sticking out from a hunting stand. He must have known the president golfs here every Friday and hid here last night. I move directly under the stand, where he can't see me, then take aim at the back of it and pull the trigger. A scream rings from the tree stand, scattering birds from nearby trees. The shooter falls from the stand with a hard thud several feet in front of me, clutching his leg in pain. I dart over to him, driving my knee into his chest and pressing the barrel of my gun to his temple.

"Don't kill me!" he cries.

Two agents rush over, pointing their guns at him. "Tell me the name of the person that hired you!" I already know the answer, but I want to hear him say it.

"It was Miles!" He sings like a canary.

"Who hired Miles?"

"I don't know!" He puts his hands in the air.

I press the gun harder into his forehead. "Not the right answer."

"Okay, okay. It was a man named Knox. That's all I know, please don't kill me."

"Do you have what you need?" I ask the agents.

They both nod and pull the guy up by his shoulders. He lets out a scream when his leg hits the ground. I walk over and stand in front of him. "One more question. Where is Miles now?"

His demeanor changes and a satisfied look covers his face. He pulls his chin up and looks directly at me. "He's on his way to Maui."

Fear chills me to my bones. I swing my gun in his direction and pull the trigger, but one of the agents grabs my arm and throws off my aim. The bullet kicks up a harmless cloud of dust from the ground next to me. "You sorry son of a bitch!" I lunge toward him and the agent has to hold me back to keep me from ripping him apart limb by limb.

"Sir, we need him alive to testify against Knox and Miles." He takes the gun out of my hand and shoves me off him.

I take off in a sprint to the clubhouse. The agents let me into the locker room, where Matthew is cleaning his wound. "Sir, I have to get to Maui. Miles is headed there after my son. Give me your phone, I need to call Brooklyn."

He hands it to me as fear fills his eyes. "I'll get one of the agents to get Air Force One on standby. It will be the quickest way for us to get there."

As I phone Brooklyn, I hear him order one of the agents to get the helicopter to land here and pick us up.

CHAPTER SIXTEEN

John

"What happened? I knew you shouldn't have gone there!" Brooklyn says as soon as she picks up the phone.

"Well, it's a good thing we did because someone just tried taking out your dad."

"What? How is that good?" Her voice has become a loud screech of anger.

"Because I tracked down the shooter and got a few answers out of him. I found out where Miles is and we have to go after him. I need you to call the nanny and tell her to lock everything down, get the supplies she needs, and take cover in the panic room."

Her sharp intake of breath is loud over the phone. "Are you sure?"

"I'm sure. Call her now, and get ready. We're going home." I hang up the phone as we're ushered to the roof.

Matthew and I walk against the wind that is whipping around us, almost knocking us over, and climb into the helicopter. Once we're buckled in, the pilot reaches back and hands us head-sets. I put mine on and look over at Matthew. "Is there a helicopter picking up Brook and Jake?"

He nods. "Should be there any minute. We'll all meet up at the private runway for our flight."

I turn away from him to watch the golf course shrink further and further into the distance, trying to remain calm even though I'm anything but. Anger surges through me, causing my heart to pound and my breathing to speed up. My jaw is clenched so tight it feels like my teeth could shatter at any moment. Sweat is beading up on my brow as I feel my face redden.

All I can think about are the moments I missed out on with my son: his birth, his first step, his first word.

I've missed it all. If Miles thinks he can take away what I have left, he's very wrong, and he's about to find out the hard way what I will do to keep my family safe.

The flight to the landing strip only takes a few minutes, but it may as well be hours to me. Matthew and I are ushered off the helicopter and toward the waiting plane. My anger and blood pressure rise with each step until all I can hear is a low ringing, drowning out everything else. I don't hear the loud sounds of helicopters and airplanes, I don't see the massive flow of people and security guards that are trying to help, I only see red. Each step I take is a determined one. I'm determined to save my son, to save my family, and put an end to Miles and his games.

Brook and Jake's helicopter hasn't arrived yet, so Matthew and I sit waiting in the airplane. Adrenaline pumps through me, causing my knees to bounce in anticipation to get on our way. Every second we sit here waiting brings Miles closer to our destination, another second closer to my son: a place I don't want him to be.

"I called the nanny and she's in code red," Brook says as she runs onto the plane and to my side.

"Did you fill her in on everything?"

She nods with tears in her eyes. I place my hands on either side of her face and direct her eyes to me. "Everything will be okay. I promise. He's not going to touch him."

She nods again as the tears finally overflow from her eyes and glide down her red cheeks.

"Okay, let's go!" Jake yells as he joins us and takes his seat.

Matthew says something to one of the guards and he heads in the direction of the cockpit.

I reach out and take Brook's hand, squeezing while rubbing my thumb over the top. The guard comes back and buckles up as the engine roars to life. I am anxious, but also filled with anticipation for this to end. My stomach feels like it's doing flips, and my legs still haven't settled. Every muscle in my body is fully tensed, refusing to relax.

When we're up in the air and the plane quiets down, the seatbelt sign kicks off. I remove my seatbelt and stand. "Anyone need a drink?"

The guard stands. "I'll get everyone a round." He quickly walks away and I begin pacing.

I look at Brook. "So tell me about the security you have in place."

Her eyes flash from her dad, to Jake, and then to me. "I... I don't know. Jake and my dad had it all set up."

Jake leans forward, resting his elbows on his knees. "The house is in a gated community on a private beach. There is a fifteen-foot brick wall that surrounds the property. The gate is controlled from inside the house or by passcode, and there are a dozen security cameras on the perimeter alone. There are six more around the house watching entry ways and windows."

"And what about the back gate? Does a security company come when an alarm is tripped?"

"The back gate can only be opened from the outside with a retina scan, and yes if any alarms are tripped, a direct message is sent to the security company. We set it up right, man. It's like breaking into Fort Knox - even you couldn't pull it off."

I scoff. "I doubt that. There's always a way, something is always over looked. I need the plans."

Jake rolls his eyes. "Aw man, I guess I left them in my other pants today."

I take a deep breath and grind my teeth together as I step forward, pointing my finger. "This is not the time to be joking around."

He stands up to my challenge. "Really? Do you think I'm taking this lightly? He's my nephew!"

"Alright, guys!" Brooklyn yells as she stands between us. "We all need to chill out. This isn't the time to be biting each other's heads off."

Jake throws his hands in the air. "You're right. I'm sorry." He holds out his hand to shake.

I slap mine into his. "Me too. I didn't mean to raise my voice. It's just been a shitty two years for me." I shake my head as I sit back down, hanging my head.

Brooklyn sits down next to me, rubbing my back. "Everything will be okay. We just have to stick together."

I nod, hearing what she's saying. I lift my head and look into her dark eyes before pressing a kiss to her forehead, then pull back and try my damnedest to predict what is going through Miles' head right now. He must be setting something into action. He sent someone to the club that Matthew goes to every Friday. He's been doing his research. He had to have known that I would be with him already and would save him.

I stand up and take the drink that is offered to me. I throw it back and set the empty glass down. "I got it."

Everyone perks up.

"Miles knew where Matthew would be. He knew I would be there in an attempt to keep him safe."

I look at all of them watching me while everything plays out before me. "The gunman wasn't trying to kill your dad," I say, looking directly at Brook.

"Then what was he trying to do?" Matthew asks, motioning toward his shoulder, which is currently wrapped in gauze.

I turn and look at him. "He was trying to get a message across."

His eyes squint together, not understanding.

I sit down across from him and lean in. "Okay, look. He wasn't there to kill you. He was there to *scare* you. Miles knew that I would be with you to keep anyone from hitting their mark. If that man wanted to kill you, he would have, and he would have been long gone before I could get to him. He stuck around to pass on a message."

"What message?" Brook asks.

"That Miles was going after John. He knew I would drop everything to run to Maui to save him, leaving you," I say, looking at Matthew again. "Unprotected."

I watch as their facial expressions change as they process what I've said.

"So Miles isn't really going after John?" Jake asks.

"Oh, he is, but it's to keep me busy while the next gunman goes after Matthew." I reach out and take Jake's glass, draining the rest of it. I take a deep breath and sit back. "This hit is Miles' retirement. It's enough money for him to disappear forever. He'll stop at nothing until the president is dead. He'll take out anyone in his way."

"So, what's all this mean?" Brook asks.

I look up at her. "It means John and Matthew need to be kept together. I can't keep them safe if they're in two different places. No matter where I am, he's always going to have men going after the other. We need to hunker down and keep one another safe."

I get up and pour another drink while thinking over the situation. I pace back and forth, trying to wrap my mind around Miles' way of thinking. He wants Matthew more than anything, even more than the payback he would get from taking my son. *That* he would enjoy, but taking out Matthew needs to be done as soon as possible.

He's only bringing John into this to fuck with me. He knows if push came to shove that John would be the one I would save, regardless of them both being family. John is a child. *My* child. I'd die before letting anything happen to him and Miles knows that.

He's going to try using all my weaknesses against me. He's going to try getting me out of my element, fucking with my head until I don't know which way to go. He can't win fairly and he knows that, so his only other option is to cheat any way he can. Playing by the rules has never been Miles' strong suit.

I take my seat again and lean forward, holding my glass with both hands. "We're going to need guns and ammo." I look at Matthew. "I'm going to need the blueprints of the house and the plan the security company gave you. If there is a way into that house, I'm going to find it. Miles won't wait patiently at the gate for someone to let him in. He already knows the way in if he's on his way."

The three of them look around at one another with a look of concern.

Hours later, when the plane lands, Matthew is on the phone getting everything I asked for. As much as I hate bringing everyone in on this, it's the only way it can go. If even one person is left vulnerable, Miles will use that person against me. This is the only way I can keep them all safe.

A limo pulls up outside of the airplane and we each rush into it. There is a black duffel bag in the seat. I pull it into my lap and open it, rummaging through the selection of guns and ammo inside. I start pulling out the weapons and loading them, handing one to Jake, Brooklyn, and Matthew, before taking two for myself and hiding them on my body.

Matthew hands over the tube containing the blueprints of the house and the plans for the security. I pop off the top and slide the papers out. They are big and awkward to hold, so I stretch the paper out and have Brook and Jake hold the edges while I look it over.

Every camera is clearly marked on the blueprints. "What kind of cameras are these?"

"They are nest cams. They are waterproof and have one-hundred-and-eighty-degree wide-angle lenses," Jake replies.

My finger traces around the line of the brick wall surrounding the property. It looks like there are cameras set up every couple hundred feet, pointed inside and outside the wall. I look at the back gate that goes up to the top of the wall, and follow it back around to the front. "What's this?" I ask, pointing at a figure on the right side of the house, outside the wall.

Brook looks a little closer. "Oh, that's a massive Banyan tree. I didn't have the heart to cut it down when we had the wall built."

"Has this tree been trimmed, or are the branches coming over the top of the wall?"

"It's huge, of course it tops the wall. Why?"

"Because," I tap the paper. "This is how they're coming in."

"They're going to climb the tree? They will still be caught on camera," Brook says.

"They don't care if they're caught on camera. If they can get in, they can shoot out the cameras and destroy the evidence. All they're looking for is a way in."

Everyone falls quiet as I roll up the papers and place them back into the tube. A part of me settles down now that I am familiar with the house and know which direction they will be coming from... if they haven't beat us there already, that is.

While we wait out the rest of the drive, I reach over and hold Brook's hand, hoping to ease any negative thoughts she may be having right now.

———

WE PULL UP AT THE GATE OUTSIDE OF THE HOUSE AND Brook leans over me to punch in the code. The gate slowly slides open on its track and the limo starts forward. I look around the property. It's covered in massive trees that provide plenty of shade and places to hide.

The limo drives around the red brick circular drive and parks in front of the main doors. "Damn, looks like the cure to cancer lined your pockets nicely," I joke, trying to break up the tension.

Brook smacks me in the chest with the back of her hand. "What's the plan? Do we just get out and walk to the door? What if they start shooting?"

"Secure the perimeter," the president orders his men.

The two guards in the limo with us exit with guns drawn and walk around, checking the trees and around corners. Within minutes, they're back. "The perimeter is secure, sir." They stand outside the car, waiting for us.

Brook pulls her keys from her purse and moves to get out. I put my hand on her shoulder to stop her. "Give me the keys. Let me make sure the house is safe before you go in there."

Her dark eyes meet mine. They hold a look I can't place. "Everything will be fine, remember?"

She nods before pressing her lips to mine. When she pulls away, she drops the keys into my hand.

I look around at her, Jake, and Matthew before stepping out. I slowly walk to the door and slide in the key. The lock turns easily. I cock the gun and hold it steady in front of me, slowly pushing the door open.

CHAPTER SEVENTEEN

John

The house is silent, apart from my feet hitting the dark wood floor. Without saying a word, I motion for the two agents to check downstairs. Brooklyn, Jake, and Matthew are all walking behind me with their guns outstretched.

I know from the blueprints that the safe room is just off the nursery, which is at the end of the long hallway upstairs. We take slow, deliberate steps with cautious movements. Halfway up the stairs, Brooklyn touches my shoulder from behind me.

"Be careful of that one, it squeaks," she whispers. I nod and step over it. I wait at the top landing for all of them to move up the staircase. All the doors leading into bedrooms are shut. I stop at the first

one, which would be the guestroom. I position
Matthew and Jake on either side of the door frame
and Brooklyn behind her father, but not without a
deep scowl crossing her face. I slowly turn the knob,
opening the door. First thing, as always, is to check
behind the door, then the closet. The three of them
enter the room and check everything else, leaving no
stone unturned. I even open the air vent to make
sure the tiny little bastard didn't find a way to fit
inside of it.

I scan the room for bugs, just to be sure. Once the
room is secure, we move on to the next room: Brooklyn's master suite. We follow the same pattern with
Jake and Matthew on either side of the door, but this
time I feel Brooklyn's finger looped in my belt. She
squints her eyes at me when I suggest she moves.
Damn woman doesn't listen.

I open the door and check behind it. Nothing. Jake
checks the walk-in closet and Matthew, the large
bathroom that's big enough to be a room all its own.
A large king-size bed, covered in silk bedding, looms
in the middle of the room. Brooklyn bends down,
checking under it. I'm caught staring at the pictures
on her bedside table. There is one of her and I that
she must have snapped when we were in the Keys.

She looks so happy. I pick up the one next to it in the blue frame. It's a picture of John right after he was born. My eyes fill with tears as I stare at it, thinking of the time I never got to spend with him. I kiss the tip of my index finger and place it on the picture before I put it back down. Brooklyn's arm goes around my waist. When she lifts her head to look at me, her eyes are glistening with tears. She reaches up and wipes one of mine away as it rolls down my cheek.

We leave the master suite, heading for the nursery. I am stopped dead in my tracks at what I see behind the door – a life-sized cardboard Superman standing in the corner, face covered with a picture of mine. Brooklyn wraps her arms around my waist from behind. "I can't believe you did this." My voice cracks as I hold back a sob.

"I wanted him to know his daddy was a superhero." She kisses my shoulder blade. She then walks over to the bookshelf and pulls out a mock set of books, displaying a number pad. She punches in the numbers and the bookshelf recesses into the wall. She walks inside and I stand staring, afraid to move. I can't believe I'm about to meet my son for the very first time.

After several tense moments of waiting, she returns carrying our son. His hair is a beautiful chocolate color, and he has Brooklyn's deep dark eyes. I fall to my knees in awe. Jake's hand rests on my shoulder. Brooklyn sets him down in front of me. He cocks his little head to one side and a smile covers his beautiful little face.

"Dada!" he yells and his arms go flying around my neck. I pull him tight, squeezing too hard but afraid to let go. I kiss the top of his head over and over again.

"I love you, J-Man," is all I can manage to as the tears stream down my face. Brooklyn joins us on the floor in a hug. I look up and see Jake wiping his face. Matthew is standing off to the side with a smile plastered to his face.

As much as I want this moment to last forever, I need to make sure the grounds are secure. I pick him up and stand, handing him back to his mother. "I need to finish checking the house. Take him back in the safe room until I'm done." I ruffle his hair and lean in to kiss Brooklyn. "I'll be back." She introduces me to Grace, the nanny, before I walk away. "Thank you for taking such good care of him."

She nods and shakes my hand.

"You need to go in there with them, sir." I tell Matthew. I watch as the three of them go back in the safe room and the door closes behind them. Jake follows me down the stairs and into the kitchen.

"This place looks like it was built for a master chef." I touch the hanging pot holder over the bar. "Nice gas stove, too."

"You know how much Brooklyn likes to eat, so she had to learn how to cook." Jake shrugs.

One agent is standing outside the back door, already on guard. He opens it when he sees me through the glass. "This area is secure," he says.

It opens up onto a pool deck with a cabana off to the side. The entire pool area is surrounded by white vinyl fencing. Cameras are perched on each corner post. I smile, thinking about Brooklyn and John splashing around in the pool. I walk back in, straight to the office where the footage from the cameras can be seen.

"Is this live feed?" I sit down in the brown leather chair. Jake takes the cushioned chair across from me.

"Yes, but you can scroll back in time." He pulls the computer screen toward him. "This button right here allows you to scroll and put multiple frames up at one time."

I click on it and open up a screen for every camera. Scrolling backward a day, I don't see anything suspicious. I make sure to focus on the tree as an access point. The leather chair creaks as I lean back. "He's not been here yet." I pick up a pencil and anxiously rock it back and forth between my fingers.

"Do you think he was waiting for you?" Jake laces his hands behind his head.

"I think so. He wants all of us here, thinking I can't protect everyone. We need to take turns watching these monitors. I want one guard out front and one in the back at all times. Matthew told me on the way here that he would have several more agents flown in to help rotate them out."

"We should probably go let them out of the safe room," he points out.

"I'll go, you stay here and keep an eye on things." I throw the pencil down on the desk and get up. He slides into my chair. "Thank you, for everything you've done for them and for stepping in to take care of John."

"Get out of here. Don't go getting all mushy on me now." He waves his hand for me to get away.

I walk through the French doors of the office and hear him call back to me. "John."

"Yeah," I look back.

"I love them, and you're welcome."

"I know, man." I take the stairs two at a time. Removing the books, I punch in the code that I saw Brooklyn push. I'm wondering if it's John's birthday.

"It's about time you let us out of here!" Brooklyn is fussing as the door opens. She runs directly into my arms. "Has he been here?"

"No. I think he is waiting on us." Matthew walks out holding John's hand. I bend down and scoop him up. "Hi, little guy. Do you want to play? I see some really cool cars over there." I point to a shelf. He nods his head.

"You two play, I'll make us all some dinner," Brooklyn says, kissing both her men on the cheek.

"I have some phone calls I need to make to check on the status of the extra agents' arrival." Matthew follows Brooklyn out of the room.

I grab the clear case holding the cars and sit down with him on the floor. A rug with a race track woven into it covers the floor in the middle of the room. I dump out all the cars and put them in front of him. "Do you have a favorite?"

His hair flops in his eyes as he reaches for a big black monster truck.

"Ah, good choice. I would have picked that one too." He looks at it and then at me. He holds his little hand out to give me the truck. "That's okay little man, you keep it. I'll pick another one."

We play for about an hour before Brooklyn peeks her head around the door with a big smile on her face.

"What?"

"It's time to eat." She's still grinning from ear to ear. She picks him up off the floor and I stand, taking him from her.

"I'm not willing to let him out of my arms yet." I brush the back of my hand down her cheek. He yawns and lays his head on my shoulder. Kissing the top of his head, I take Brooklyn's hand in mine and we walk down the stairs to the kitchen. "Damn woman, it smells good in here."

"Nothing fancy. I put together some homemade pizzas."

"Pizza." The little man perks up.

"It's his favorite." She takes him from me and sets him in a booster seat strapped to the chair and buckles him in. I sit in the chair next to him.

"Where is everyone?"

"Dad is held up in the office and Jake went home to grab a few things."

"Did he go by himself?" I ask as she places a plate in front of me.

"No. Some more agents arrived and one of them went with him." She has a small plate with cut-up pizza on it. She places it in front of John and he digs in with both hands.

"I guess he has his mother's appetite," I tease with her. I take a big bite and cheese drips down my chin. "This is really good."

"Did you doubt me?" She laughs and sits down across from me.

I look over at J-Man and see that he already has pizza sauce in his hair. "How did he do that?" I point.

"Wait until you see him eat spaghetti."

"This seems so normal. A man could get used to this." As I polish off the rest of my pizza, Brooklyn's foot slides up my pant leg.

"I love that you're finally home. I know you will be a good dad." She can't quit smiling at me.

"We'll have to have a few more of these rug rats." I look over and J-Man's face is in his plate. He's fallen asleep. "Does he do that a lot?" I chuckle.

"You wore him out. I need to give him a bath before I put him to bed."

"Can I help?"

"Sure you can." She gets up and takes our plates to the sink. I walk up behind her and place a kiss on her shoulder.

"You cooked, I'll clean after we get him cleaned up."

"We'll worry about them tomorrow. I have other things planned for your first night in our house."

"Mmm... I like your idea better."

"Please tell me you left me some food, I'm starving," Jake's voice blares from behind us.

"It's in the oven. Go see if my Dad is off the phone yet so that he can eat too. We're going upstairs to bathe J-Man. Show my dad where everything is, please."

I pick him up out of his plate and carry him upstairs to the bathroom. Brooklyn fills the tub with warm water and bubbles. "I wouldn't mind one of those when he's in bed."

"What? A bubble bath?" She laughs.

"I haven't had one since I was a kid. I bet those jets would make a lot of bubbles."

"I'll add that to our plans tonight." She wakes him and undresses him in my arms. I kneel down by the tub and scoop up a handful of bubbles to blow at her. "You're such a toddler."

"Good, then he and I will get along really well." I splash water at him and he splashes me back. In the end, I end up as wet as he is.

CHAPTER EIGHTEEN
John

$\mathcal{I}$ lift John out of the bathtub while Brooklyn wraps a towel around him. She drains the tub and I follow her into his bedroom, sitting in the middle of the floor to dry him off while she gathers his clothes.

"Here, smear some of this on him. I like him baby fresh," she says, handing me a bottle of pink baby lotion.

I look at it and scoff. "Why is it pink?"

She shrugs while pulling clothes out of his dresser. "It's just baby lotion. Pink doesn't mean it's only for girls."

I open the bottle and smell it. "It even smells pink!"

She giggles and holds out her hand for the lotion. I roll my eyes and squirt the lotion into my palm before rubbing him down with it.

When the lotion is on, I wipe my hands down my pants, unable to stand the greasy feeling on my skin. Brooklyn hands me a diaper.

I take it and study it for a minute. I turn it around and back before unfolding it.

"We're starting to potty-train him but he still needs a diaper at night," she says, placing her finger in his hand. He giggles and tries chewing on her. "He's also cutting his molars."

"I don't blame him. I'd like to bite you too, just not your finger," I tease while still trying to figure out the diaper.

She reaches out and takes it from me. "Let me show you." She takes his ankles in her hands and lifts him up while sliding the diaper under him at the same time. The next thing I know, the diaper is on and he's sitting up.

"How did you do that so fast?"

She grins. "Lots of practice. This little man used to make a dirty diaper every time he ate. We've gone through a ton of diapers." She pulls his shirt over his head and he slides his arms through.

When he's dressed, I pick him up and cradle him close to my body. I inhale his scent and kiss his forehead while rocking him to sleep.

Brooklyn leans against the door frame, shaking her head. "You are going to spoil him," she practically sings.

"I can't help it. I don't want to ever let him go."

She walks over and kisses his head before kissing my lips. "When you're done with your bonding, I'll be in the bedroom." She walks out quietly, flipping off the light as she walks by.

I hold him a little tighter and rock him a little slower. I look down at him and his eyes lock on mine. He looks so much like the both of us, but his dark eyes are all Brooklyn's. He raises his hand to my cheek and says, "Dada."

"That's right, and I'll be here with you always, little man," I whisper as I watch his eyes flutter closed.

A warmth spreads through me, starting at my heart and flowing throughout my whole body. I know it's the love I already feel for this little guy I helped create. I don't know how something so perfect came from me, but there is one thing I *do* know: I would stop at nothing to make sure he is always safe and taken care of.

Just as I go to lie him down, his arms jump and scare him into waking up. He sticks out his bottom lip and starts to whine. I start the rocking process all over while humming the tune to *Stand By Me*. "One day, I'll teach you the words to the song," I whisper.

Before I even hit the chorus, he's fast asleep. I move a little slower this time to put him in bed. I pull the blanket up around him and back away slowly without ever taking my eyes off him.

I walk into the bedroom and close the door behind me. When I turn around, I expect to find Brooklyn but instead find an empty room. "Brook?" I call out.

"In here," she says from the bathroom.

I follow the sound of her voice and find her up to her chin in bubbles in the old claw-foot bathtub.

"I know you wanted the jets, but my tub is bigger. Big enough for the two of us. What do ya say?"

I begin pulling off my clothes, hoping that's enough of an answer.

I slide in behind her and she leans against my chest. "I never thought I would have this."

"Have what?" I ask.

"Have you, here with our family in this house. I thought you were gone. I wished every time that John did something cute that you could see it. Every night I crawled into bed alone, every morning I woke up alone. You were all I thought about." She spins around to face me. "And here you are. If I had known…"

"Shh, I know. You couldn't have known." I sit up and place my hand on the side of her face. "I thought of you every minute I was locked up. You're what kept me going."

She grins.

"What?"

She rolls her eyes. "I was just wondering if you thought of me the same way I thought of you."

I feel my eyebrows draw together. "What do you mean?"

She leans in, lips grazing my ear as she whispers, "I used to fantasize about you while I touched myself."

Her words turn me on instantly. "Oh, I thought about it. I just couldn't do anything about it." I pull away and see her flushed cheeks. "Are you going to show me?"

Her eyes pop open. "Show you?"

I nod, slowly. "Mm-hmm. I want to see how you touch yourself while you think about me."

She offers up a shy smile before standing. I watch as the bubbles roll off of her naked body. They glide over the swell of her breasts, down her flat stomach, and over her round ass.

I can't take my eyes off her as she steps from the tub and covers herself with a towel. I pull the drain from the tub and wrap a towel around my waist before following her back into the bedroom. I stand back, watching as she pulls the blankets back and takes her place on the bed.

Her dark eyes lock onto mine as her hand travels from her breast, down her stomach, and stops at the junction between her legs. Her lips part and a sigh leaves them.

I'm still standing by the bathroom door, unable to move or do anything but watch her. When she lets out a soft moan, a spark shoots directly to my stomach and lights every nerve ending. I'm rock hard from watching her touch herself, and knowing that it's me she's thinking about only makes me want to touch her more.

I no longer have control over my body. My feet begin pulling me forward until I find myself crawling onto the bed. I push away her hand and replace it with my mouth.

"I thought you wanted to watch me?" she whispers.

"As sexy as that is, I want to be the one that makes you come. You're mine." I double my efforts until she is grasping the sheets and calling my name.

Her sounds, her movements, her taste... it all just makes me that much harder. I can't wait until I can sink deep inside her.

"My turn to taste you," she says, pushing me away.

I don't even have time to decline before she's sucking me into her mouth. My eyes roll to the back of my head as a groan escapes me. I'm painfully hard and I know it will only be a matter of minutes before I'm spilling every last drop into her hot mouth. "You have to stop, Brook. I don't want to finish yet."

As if she hadn't heard my words at all, she takes me deeper into her mouth. I no longer have control over my voice, I can't deny her. I place my hand on her shoulder, hoping she backs away so I can take my time with her, but she digs her nails into my thighs. The little bit of pain mixes with the pleasure and I can no longer hold back. I let myself go, spilling into her mouth with a loud moan.

My heart is pounding, my breathing is rapid, and we're both covered in a light sheen of sweat that glistens under the bedside lamp. Brooklyn lays back against the pillows, parting her legs with me sitting between them.

"Think you can go again?" she asks, sticking out her chest just a bit more.

I feel myself harden from the view of her spread out before me and I move to cover her body with mine.

I kiss her passionately, wanting, *needing* to feel her. Needing to remind myself that this is real, and this is what the rest of my life could look like. Her hands glide down my biceps as she reaches around me. Her nails bite into my lower back as she lifts her hips toward me.

I pull back only slightly. "Are you in a hurry?" I grin.

She nods. "I want you inside of me now, John."

My lips crash into hers. As our tongues twist together, I push forward, sliding into her. She's so hot and tight around me. I pull back, only to thrust back inside her, hitting that little spot that always sends her spiraling.

I feel her tighten around me, almost bringing me over the edge with her, but I hold back. I want so much more.

Her legs wrap around me tightly as her lips find mine. She moans against them while I take everything I want and give everything I am.

When I feel her orgasm end, I let mine go with a powerful growl, pumping into her hard and fast until I can no longer move.

We both collapse, holding on to one another while we try to regulate our erratic breathing.

She trails her nails down my back and up again. "My toes are numb." She giggles.

"Was that better than what you imagined?" I pull back to study her expression.

"So much better." Her eyes are so heavy, she can't hold them open. They flutter closed and I pull out of her. I rest on my side and pull her against my chest. As my breathing and heart rate slow, I drift off to sleep.

———

"YOU'LL NEVER GET HER BACK," MILES SAYS AS HE LANDS *a solid hit to my jaw. "If you know what's best for you, you'll take the deal I'm offering." Another hit to the face.*

My eyes start to roll back as unconsciousness threatens to take over.

"Oh, no you don't," he says before slapping me across the face.

My head is pounding from the beating it's already taken, but the slap brings me back. My eyes focus on the short, round man that's standing in front of me. Anger washes over me and I use it to hang on, to give me the strength I need to survive another beating.

———

I WAKE BUT DON'T BOTHER TO OPEN MY EYES TO THE bright room. I can still feel the hits like they just happened. I reach across the bed, hoping to find her. I need her. I need to feel her to confirm that she is here and she is mine, that I'm finally away from Miles and the years of torture I had to endure, but the bed is cold and empty.

I force my eyes open and sit up, looking around the room. I rub the sleep from my eyes before I stand and pull on a pair of sweat pants. I stumble through the brightly lit room toward the kitchen.

Brook is singing and dancing in front of the stove

while my little man is clapping and giggling. I lean against the door frame and watch them for a moment. This is the most normal I've ever felt in my life, and I know it's only a matter of time before this is shattered too.

"Good morning," Brook says, looking up at me without stopping her dancing.

"Good morning." I lean over and kiss Little Man on the head and close the distance between Brooklyn and me. I pull her against my chest and our eyes meet. "I guess you wore me out last night."

She blushes under my stare. "If it makes you feel any better, I must have worn myself out too. John woke me up screaming for food." She turns and looks at him longingly. "He really does take after me."

I laugh and swat her ass. "Make your men some breakfast, woman."

Her eyes cut to me. She's trying to give me a serious look, but I can see her trying to hide the smile that's trying to form.

I pour myself a cup of coffee and sit down next to John. "How are you today, buddy?"

He smiles and giggles while clapping his hands. "Mom, mom, mom." He reaches for her.

"Are you trading me in already?" I tease.

Brook turns around. "Ha, he doesn't want me. He just wants the bacon in my hand. That kid is a bacon eating machine." She picks up a piece of bacon from the plate and tears off a small bit. He looks ready to attack her as she hands it over. His jaws are chomping before he's even got the bacon to his mouth.

I laugh. "Yep, he takes after you."

"Don't be mean to my nephew. He can't help it if he got his mom's eating habits," Jake says, walking into the kitchen and stealing a piece of bacon.

Brook looks him up and down. "Or maybe it's from his uncle who hasn't stopped gaining weight." She pats his stomach.

Jake looks down at his stomach. "I'm not fat." He raises his shirt to show off his six pack.

I laugh and shake my head. "Alright, put that away before you make us all lose our appetite."

Jake flips me off before turning around to pour his coffee. I look over at Little J, who's now holding up his middle finger, and I bust out laughing.

"What?" both of them say as they spin around to see John flipping off the room.

Jake's laugh is as loud as mine but Brooklyn doesn't look happy. She turns toward Jake, ready to smack him with the spatula.

Jake dodges and runs behind me.

Brook points the spatula at him. "You're going to turn my sweet little baby into a sailor!"

I look back at John, who has long forgotten about the use of his middle finger. Instead, he's playing with a set of keys.

"He's forgotten all about it. See?" Jake says, motioning toward J-Man.

She looks at him and her smile forms. Her eyes cut back to Jake and the smile leaves. "You're lucky!"

"Yeah, yeah," Jake mumbles as he moves to sit down on the other side of John. "Boy am I glad you're back. I don't know how much longer I could've handled her." He looks at me. "You've got your work cut out for you."

I shrug. "It helps that I get to sleep with her."

Brook's dad walks in and heads straight to the coffee pot. All talk stops.

He takes a seat just as Brooklyn is placing bacon and pancakes on the table. John throws the keys on the floor and tries crawling out of his seat to get the food.

"Chill, little man. I won't let you starve." I stand and make his plate, cutting the food up into tiny pieces like I saw Brooklyn do last night.

I cover everything in syrup and set it in front of him.

"Just so you know, *you're* giving him a bath," Brooklyn says.

"Huh?" I ask confused. "How many baths does the kid need?"

"It's going to take twenty minutes to get all that syrup out of his hair."

I turn and look over at him. He sticks his hand in the syrup and licks it. Suddenly, he's crazy-eyed and shoving food into his mouth. When he's out of room, he decides to just smear the syrup all over his body in hopes of absorbing it through the top of his head and face.

I grab a pancake and wipe the syrup off his cheek with it before taking a bite. "This parenting thing won't be that bad."

CHAPTER NINETEEN

John

"*D*amn, I didn't think I'd ever get all the syrup out of Little Man's hair," I say, walking into the garage with Jake.

"You said we had a project. What is it?" He hops on the counter and starts messing with the hanging tools.

I reach in my pocket and remove the bullet I took from Miles' drawer. "We need to make this fit in my gun." I show him one of my bullets to compare it to.

He takes it out of my hand and examines it closely. "I think we could shave it down a little bit to make it work. Your only other option is to have a gun made specifically for it."

"I don't think Miles is going to give us that kind of time." I walk over to my motorcycle - the one that Brooklyn has claimed as her own - and straddle my leg over the seat. Jake takes the keys off a hook and dangles them at me.

"If she catches you on that bike, you won't have to worry about Miles killing you. She'll do it with her bare hands," he taunts me, hanging the keys back up.

"I'm not afraid of her. This is my damn bike." I hear the door start to open and immediately jump off the bike.

"What are you boys doing out here?" Brooklyn's head peeks out the door.

"Nothing," I answer quickly. Jake chuckles. I reach around and smack him.

She opens the door wider and points her finger at me. "Don't be getting any ideas about that bike, mister." She slams the door.

"I'm not afraid of her," Jake mumbles, laughing.

I punch him in the arm. "Shut the hell up!"

"Hey, you better be nice to me if you want my help," he says, rubbing his arm.

I walk around the room, opening up drawers to look for anything we can use to shave the bullet. I find what I need and walk back over to Jake. He holds it on the counter while I work on it. Several minutes later, the door opens again. This time it's Matthew.

"What are you two up to?" he asks, making his way toward us.

Jake holds the bullet up into the air and I give him a dirty look. "Making this fit in John's gun so he can kill Miles." I want to fucking kill Jake for saying that in front of him.

"I..." I stammer.

Matthew holds his hand in the air to stop me from saying anything. "I want him gone as much as you do. Every day he breathes, he's a threat to my family and the men and women that work for me." He places a firm grip on my shoulder. "Just promise me when this is finally over, you will give up this job for good."

"I gave it up the day I met Brooklyn. I don't *want* to kill Miles, I *have* to. He's not given me any other choice."

"I know that, son. Is there anything I can help you with?" He takes the bullet from Jake's hand and looks at it closely.

"I think you've helped enough by giving us security. I'm sure I've made your political career hell already."

"My ratings are good, don't worry about my career." He hands the bullet back to me. "One day, maybe, when I'm no longer president, you could teach me how to make bullets."

"Really?" I'm astonished that he wants to know how, much less have me teach him something.

"Yes, really. Once upon a time, I loved to go to the range and shoot." He pats me on the back and walks to the doorway. "Carry on boys, I have some phone calls to make.

"Wow, he's a pretty cool dude," Jake says.

"Yeah, he is. Anyone else would have shot me for even coming *close* to their daughter. The fact that he accepts me for who I've been says a lot. Brooklyn adores him."

"Well, he raised one hell of a woman. I still can't believe of all people, she picked you." He laughs and punches me back.

"Me either man."

———————

AFTER DINNER AND LITTLE JOHN IS IN BED, WE ALL meet in the living room. While everyone else is sitting on the couch and chairs, I'm standing, pacing the floor in front of them.

"Miles could show up at any time. I want us to be ready. I think Brooklyn, Matthew, and Little John should sleep in the safe room. I don't want to be alerted that he's on the grounds and have to scramble to keep you all safe. We have extra agents on hand now. I'll set one up in the nursery so that he's right outside the safe room."

"What about Jake?" Brooklyn asks.

"Jake will be near me at all times. I need the extra hands and eyes." He nods in understanding.

"There are already a couple of cots set up in there. I'll go get another one from the garage." Brooklyn stands.

"You go nowhere by yourself." I motion for one of the agents to go with her. "An agent is monitoring the cameras at all times. One is outside the gate, one at the front door, and one in the back. But, I want Miles to step foot on the property. That way I have just cause to shoot him. But I don't want to kill him here."

"What? Why not?" Jake is on his feet.

"I don't want his death to happen here at this house. I'll shoot him with the tracking bullet and when he flees, we'll go after him. One of the agents was able to install the software we need to track him down."

Jake sits back down. "I guess that makes sense."

"It doesn't to me." Brooklyn bursts back into the room. "I want that bastard dead, not give him a chance to get away!" She's got steam coming out of her ears.

"He won't get away this time."

She closes the distance between us and gets in my face. "I'm not willing to risk that!" Her jaw is clenched and she's breathing hard.

I reach out to touch her shoulder and she swats my hand away. "I promise he won't get away again."

"You weren't the one who had to rebuild your life without the man you loved. You didn't have to raise a child on your own and face every day alone!" She turns and stomps off up the stairs. The bedroom door slams hard and echoes through the house.

"I don't think I've ever seen her that mad," Jake mutters.

"Me either," Matthew says.

"Um... I think our meeting is over. But nothing has changed." I walk toward the stairs.

"Other than the fact that you may have no balls left if you go up there." Jake laughs.

I ignore his banter in fear that he may be right. I pace in front of the door a few times. I've faced down evil and never showed any fear. How come this five-foot-eleven-inch tall redhead scares the hell out of me? *I'm the man, I wear the pants in this family, right? I can do this*. I give myself a pep talk, then adjust myself, looking down, "It's okay boys, don't listen to Jake. We got this."

I push through the door but don't see her. A rustling sound drifts over from the walk-in closet. "Brook." I call her name, but she doesn't answer. Clothes start flying out of the closet. A blouse hits me in the face as I walk closer.

"What are you doing?" I pull it off my face.

"I'm straightening. What does it look like?" she snaps without looking up at me.

"Is this what you do when you're angry?" I step inside with her.

"It's better than what I wanted to do to you." She finally stops and looks at me.

I step closer and wrap my arms around her. "Thank you for not doing whatever that was." I feel her relax into my arms. "I'm doing this for us. I don't want death here. I don't want you to remember his body lying dead anywhere on this property. I'm sorry you had to rebuild your life without me. I'm sorry that you had to have John on your own. You know I would have given anything to be here with you."

She releases the clothes that are in her hands and wraps her arms around my neck. "I know. I'm sorry I said those things. I just hate the thought of him getting away."

"You have to trust me. He won't. If I have to track him to the ends of the earth, I will."

"What about Knox? What is going to keep him from hiring someone else to hunt you down?"

"With the confession of one of Miles' men and all the dirt we have on him, all his assets have been frozen. Thanks to your dad. He's also been sent to a maximum security prison. He will have no contact with the outside world. He's lost all his rights and he'll be locked away for a very long time."

She smiles and then pouts her bottom lip. "What else?" I ask.

"I don't like sleeping without you."

I draw her in and kiss her softly a few times. "When this is over, we will never have to be apart again." I take her hands and drop down on one knee. "Will you marry me and make me the happiest man and father on this earth? I don't have a ring, but you can have whatever you want."

She gets down on the floor with me. "I don't need a ring. I only need you and J-Man. And maybe another baby," she adds, with a smile that could light up the world.

"Is that a yes, then?" I stare into her eyes.

"Yes, I will marry you." She grabs my hair and pulls me in for a kiss.

"I love you, Brooklyn."

"I love you, too. Now let's go break the news to my dad." She drags me off the floor with her.

"He won't be surprised. He gave me his permission."

———

Brooklyn, Matthew, and J-Man are all asleep in the safe room. I can't sleep in that big king-sized bed alone, so I head downstairs to make myself a bourbon, neat. Jake is already sitting at the bar top, working on a drink.

"What are you doing up?" I walk behind the bar and grab a glass.

"My mind kept racing with everything that's happened and I couldn't fall asleep."

"It will all be over soon and we can all get a good night's rest."

"I sure hope you're right."

An agent walks into the room and interrupts our conversation. "Sir, someone dressed in black and smoking a cigarette has been spotted outside the gate near the tree." He places the open laptop on the bar and pushes it in my direction. Jake comes around to where I'm standing.

"Is that him?" He looks closely at the screen.

"That's the little Napoleon. I would recognize him anywhere."

CHAPTER TWENTY

John

My heart rate increases and my chest swells with anger. "Let's go."

I tuck the gun with the special bullet in the waistband of my jeans and grab another gun, just in case he has someone with him. If I know Miles, he didn't come alone. He probably has men surrounding us right now.

Jake picks up a gun from the table and follows me to the back door. "Tell your men to surround the house. Nobody gets inside. Do you hear me?"

The guard nods and rushes off to spread the word.

Jake and I step out into the darkness beyond the door. I stick close to the wall, letting my eyes adjust.

There are no lights, aside from the moon and thousands of twinkling stars overhead. There is no wind blowing and other than the crashing waves of the ocean, no sounds. Everything is deathly quiet, like the world is preparing for all this to end.

Once I'm at the corner of the wall, I peek around the side of the house and look up at the branches of the tree, which are rustling and dropping leaves into the yard despite the windless night. I focus my eyes and see his round ass dangling from a branch, too afraid to let go and take the fall required to set foot on the property.

I shake my head. And he thought this would actually work? I want to laugh to myself, but I hold it back. Miles is a lot dumber that I ever gave him credit for.

I step away from the house and motion for Jake to stay back. I don't want Miles to know he's there and waiting.

I aim my gun up in the tree and cock it. The sound of the bullet going into the chamber cuts through the night. Miles stops moving, knowing he's caught.

"Why don't you get down from there so we can settle this once and for all."

"Don't shoot. I just want to talk," he says with exasperation in his voice.

"Then talk."

He shimmies his way down the branch and lets go, falling a couple of feet. He lands with a thud on the ground. If my family wasn't in danger, I'd laugh. It's like a bad comedy.

"What made you think that this plan would work, Miles? I mean, I'm a trained hitman. You of all people should know there's no sneaking around me."

He brushes off his pants and stands up straight, holding his hands out in front of him. "I'm not even packing heat. I have a new deal for you."

This time, I do laugh. I shake my head while never taking my eyes or the gun off him. "No more deals. This is done."

In the distance, I hear gunfire. I want to run to check it out, but Miles here is more important. "Who's that? How many did you bring with you?"

He laughs, a deep menacing sound. "You didn't really think I'd come alone, did you?"

I shake my head. "I knew you wouldn't, but there isn't anything happening here tonight. Everyone is locked up safe, far away from you."

Miles begins pacing back and forth slowly with his arms behind his back. "I have to say, I'm proud of you. I never thought you'd have the balls to do what you've done."

"And what's that?"

"I really expected you to leave the president and come rescue your boy. I never thought you'd drag everyone along with you."

"I know how that fucked up mind of yours works. Did you really think you'd just walk right out of here? You invaded my territory. I've been waiting for this moment. I'm prepared for anything you can throw my way. Let's finish this."

"As you wish." Miles jumps and tackles me to the ground, knocking the gun from my hand. I turn to look at Jake, he's passed out on the ground. How'd that happen? I didn't hear anything.

Miles is on top of me, delivering blow after blow to my face. I roll him off me and straddle him. I wrap my hands around his throat and begin squeezing. He's fighting me with every ounce of strength he has, but I have surrendered myself to the whirlwind of rage in my chest. I cannot be stopped.

Gunshots continue ringing out around us. A guard rushes to Jake's side. Miles' eyes are beginning to close and I squeeze a little harder. Just as the life is about to leave his body, something hits me in the back of the head and I fall forward, losing control of my body. My eyesight blurs.

I'm on my back looking up. All I can see is the dark silhouette of the tree branches blowing in the wind. I shake my head, trying to get my vision back to normal as I climb to my feet. The night is filled with the smell of gunpowder and the sounds of combat. With my blurred vision, it is impossible to tell who is who. I look back at the ground, but Miles is no longer there.

I run over to Jake and slap him across the face. He groans but comes to. "What the hell happened?"

"I don't know, but I've lost Miles. Get up!" I help him to his feet and push him one direction while I go another.

I run toward the front of the house and see Miles and three of his men are standing by the front gate, which is now open. I stop, studying them. What's happening? They're leaving?

"I'll be back for you, John," Miles says as he holds up his right hand. It is holding some sort of little controller. His thumb presses down on a button at the top, and an explosion shatters the night air behind me. The base of the house erupts in flames. Windows explode outward, showering the lawn with shards of glass. The force of the explosion blows the front door from its hinges. I turn back to look at Miles, but he's running off.

I look at the house and then to him again. I have to get my shot off, but I need to check on my family and get them out of the burning house.

"Fuck!" I scream as I chase after him, hoping that Jake can get in the house and help them. I follow him out of the gate and see him nearing a black Hummer. I pull the gun from my waistband, aiming instinctively and pulling the trigger. The gun fires loudly and the bullet shoots from the barrel, cutting through the air until it lodges deep into the back of his shoulder. He screams and stumbles forward, turning back to glare at me after catching his balance.

I can see the anger on his face from here, but he won't come back and I know it. I take my leave and run back to the house. I have to get them out.

I run in through the busted front door and dash through the flames and up the stairs. I rush into John's room and open the safe room. Flames are quickly devouring everything in sight, the smoke choking the air.

"Come on! We have to get out!" I yell as they start filing out of the safe room. I grab one of John's baby blankets and hand it to Brooklyn to wrap around him. He's kicking and screaming from the explosion, the heat, and smoke.

I lead them down the stairs and out to the back yard. Brooklyn crumbles to her knees at the end of the property. She looks up, and the bright flames light up her face. I can hear the fire truck and ambulance sirens in the distance, getting closer.

"Did you get your shot?" Jake asks.

"Yeah, I got it," I answer, looking up at the flames.

Three guards come running over to us. "We have him. He's on the move." He shows me the screen on his smart phone. There is a small red dot that is traveling fast away from the house.

I take the phone and turn towards Brooklyn. "I have to go."

"What? No!"

I shake my head and pull her and John against my chest. "I'm sorry. I have to... before he manages to dig that bullet out and I can't find him. I'll be back. I swear."

"You can't do this, John. Not now. Where are we supposed to go?"

"Stay together. Go to Jake's house. I'll be able to keep track of Miles."

Her eyes fill with tears. "Please come back to us. We need you."

"I will." I move in for a kiss, lingering at her lips longer than needed.

I pull away. "Get the house keys from Jake and get them out of here," I say, looking at Matthew.

He nods and pulls out his phone.

"Come on, Jake." I turn and run toward the front of the house. The firetruck is pulling into the gate as I turn and force open the garage door. Smoke rolls out but I push on.

I grab the keys to the bike from the wall and jump on, revving the engine.

When I pull out of the garage, Jake is already directing the EMTs to where everyone is waiting.

"Jake! Let's go!"

He runs over to me. "I'm not riding bitch."

"Shut up and go get on a bike," I tell him, shaking my head.

He runs into the garage as the flames begin to take over the framework. Within seconds, he's pulling up next to me. "Let's go."

I nod and shift the bike into gear, squealing the tires off the brick driveway.

I know I'm going to pay dearly for taking this bike, but it has to be done. Fuck, I'll buy her a bike instead of a ring if she wants, or both. She deserves it all after the past two years she's been through.

I turn left out of the driveway and pull the phone from my pocket. The dot is getting farther and farther away. I stop at a stop sign and mount the phone to the gas tank with the aftermarket holder. I can't believe she put this shit on here. I'll have to chew her ass out for this. I would tear the damn thing off if I didn't need it so bad right now. I shake my head while Jake laughs beside me. He knows exactly what I'm pissed about.

"Oh, come on man. We have bigger issues than the attraction you have toward your bike."

I flip him off before shifting back in gear and driving as fast as my bike will let me onto the freeway.

This ride feels like it's taking forever. I track Miles to a large hanger and watch as he gets on a plane. There are several smaller planes around and a couple large ones. It seems as though this place is being used like a small, independently owned airport.

We stash our bikes and just as the plane starts to take off, I grab an attendant and push him against the side of the building. "Where's that plane going?" I shove my gun in his face.

He holds his hands up. "Chicago. It's going to Chicago."

I grind my teeth together. "I need a plane now!"

"I can't fly. I just work here."

"Where can I find a pilot?"

He points me in the direction of the hanger. I shove my gun in his face. "If you tell anyone that you saw us here..."

He quickly shakes his head. "I won't. I swear."

I push him back, releasing him as I turn my back to him.

We walk through the open door quietly, unsure of what we will find inside. There are several planes parked next to work stations.

I lead the way along the side wall, staying out of sight by hiding behind the planes. Every few steps, I stop and listen. There is no noise. Everything is deathly quiet. I'm beginning to fear that there isn't any pilots in here. If there were, surely they would be talking or making some kind of noise.

We quietly walk through the hanger until we come to a man sitting at a wooden bar. He's holding his head in his right hand, while his left clutches a half empty glass. I point him out from our hiding spot. "There's our pilot," I whisper.

"That drunk guy?"

I shrug. "Let's just hope he isn't the one that drank that whole bottle setting in front of him.

"Do you think he will take us?"

"Only one way to find out," I say, slowly walking out of the shadows to approach the pilot. I sit down at his side. He must have been here for a while - his blue eyes are bloodshot and drooping. Suddenly I realize that he is the one that drank the bottle setting in front of him. "Are you a pilot?"

The man looks at me, confusion etching his face, causing wrinkles to form around his bloodshot eyes. "What's it to you?" he asks gruffly, annoyance dripping from his words.

"I need a ride to Chicago."

He shakes his head. "I've been drinking since noon, buddy. You don't want to get on a bicycle with me, let alone an airplane."

I lean in. "Well, you see, that's where you're wrong. Just get me back to the states. I can take it from there."

He sets his drink down with a little too much force. "Didn't you hear me? I said no!"

I show him the gun I'm carrying, poking him in the ribs with the tip. "I said get up."

His eyes zero in on the gun and he stands, walking toward the open back door. I motion for Jake and we quickly follow him out onto the runway.

"This is the only plane I have," he slurs.

The tiny plane looks like it's made of papier-mâché. Looking back at Jake, I ask, "What do you think?"

"So, let me get this straight. You want to get on this little rickety ass plane with a pilot who's been drinking all day?"

I think it over and nod. "Yeah, I think it's our only option."

He runs his hand through his hair. "What the fuck, man? Why couldn't you have just shot him back at the house? We'd still have a house right now! We wouldn't be about to die in a fiery plane crash at the hands of a drunk pilot."

I grab him by his shirt and pull him closer. "You need to get your shit under control."

He pushes away from me. "Alright, fine." He nods and starts pacing.

I turn back to the pilot. "Can you do this?"

He's leaning against the side of the plane, almost asleep. His head perks up. "Oh yeah. I've done this many times. Once, I even passed out while flying and scared the shit out of the people who paid me to fly them to Mexico."

I laugh nervously. "Yeah, great story. Let's go."

Jake's eyes are wide with fear. "I don't know about this, man. Are you sure you don't want me to stay with Brook and J-Man?"

I laugh. "Not this time, bro. You're on the front line."

CHAPTER TWENTY-ONE

John

"John, seriously, he can't even walk in a straight line." Jake continues to fuss as we board the small plane. I buckle in up front next to the pilot. Jake sits in the narrow seat in the back.

"We only have to make it to the states. After that, I know a guy in California. He'll get us to Chicago."

The plane wobbles on take-off. I focus on the instrument panel and making sure our pilot stays awake. "Why don't you get some sleep, Jake? It's going to be about a five-hour flight." I look back at him and he's holding his stomach.

"I don't feel so good." He wretches. I find a bag and hand it to him to just in time for him to barf.

"What the hell, man? You've flown a thousand times and never gotten sick."

"I've never flown with a drunk pilot that swerved all over the runway." He wretches again.

I look back over at the pilot, whose head is bobbing. "Hey man, wake up!" I shake his shoulder and his eyes pop open.

"We're going to die!" Jake is in full-out panic mode.

"Calm down. I'll fly the plane." I start to unbuckle and the plane jerks to the left. I grab the controls and straighten us back out.

"Have you ever flown a plane before?" Jake has unbuckled and he's tugging the pilot out of the way. "I'll do it!"

"You've never flown before either," I grab the pilot's feet, helping to move him out of the way. The plane jostles and my head hits the top. Before I get my bearings, Jake jumps into the pilot seat.

"I took lessons while you were away."

"Really? That's awesome." I suddenly feel much better.

"I didn't finish or pass, but I took them."

The pit in my stomach has returned with a vengeance. I'm rummaging through compartments and under seats.

"What are you looking for?" Jake's hands are firmly on the controls.

"An instruction manual."

He starts laughing.

"What's so damn funny?" I slam one of the compartments.

"They don't keep those on the plane."

"Why the hell not?"

"Well, first off, it's a private plane. Secondly, the pilot that owns it, knows how to fly it. He doesn't need the instructions." He points his thumb in the direction of the pilot passed out in the back.

I double check all my buckles, then brace myself on the dash of the plane. "We are going to die."

"Relax. Why don't you try to take a nap?" he says in a mocking tone.

"Just sit there and shut the hell up. Focus on flying the damn plane!" His lips move as he mumbles something under his breath. Every now and then he glares at me, but doesn't utter another word. I watch the phone screen, keeping an eye on the red dot that is Miles. It looks like they are about an hour ahead of us. We'll lose time stopping in California. I'm okay with lagging behind. I want him to think he wasn't followed. He would never believe that I would leave my family after he blew up the house. Honestly, I'm feeling guilty about leaving them, but if I don't take Miles out, we'll always be running and looking over our shoulders. I'd rather die myself than let my family continue to live like that.

————

"HEY, JOHN. WAKE UP. WE'RE GOING TO BE LANDING soon." Jake shakes my arm. For a minute I've forgotten where I am. The phone slid off and is laying on the floor in front of me. Once I get my whereabouts, I snatch it off the floor and start it back up, waiting for the red dot to appear. My heart stops until I see it start to flash.

"You fell asleep."

"Sorry, man." I run my hand down my face, then stretch. "We didn't die."

"No, but we haven't landed yet. That's the part I failed."

I look over at him wide-eyed with that knot suddenly back in my gut.

"Move out of my way," the pilot barks.

Jake quickly unbuckles and gets out of the way, letting him take over. "I'm glad you finally decided to join us," Jake snaps.

The pilot ignores him and starts talking over the radio, setting us up to land. A few minutes later, the landing gear grinds its way down from the belly of the plane. The runway stretches out before us, its orange lights illuminating our path. He eases back on the controls and we touch down smoothly.

We both unbuckle, grabbing our bags. "We need to run, Jake. There is no time to waste." The pilot gets out of the plane with us and I dig some cash out of my pocket.

"I'm sorry for the way I had to do this, but this is all I have. Please take it." I shove the cash into his hand. "And please take a nap before you fly home." I turn around and we both run full speed to the hangar. The pilot we're about to meet has worked for me many times and been paid very well in the process. He's an old cranky guy, but the best damn pilot I've ever met.

We are both out of breath by the time we make it to the open door. The sun has started to rise, giving us enough light to see inside. In the very back, Joe is pouring himself a mug of coffee.

"Joe!" I yell, and he turns in my direction.

The man has millions of dollars, yet only has about four teeth in his entire mouth. "What brings you here?" He smiles and heads in my direction.

"Sorry, Joe. No time for pleasantries. I need to get to Chicago."

"You know the deal."

"The money will be in your account tomorrow."

"Good enough for me." He pulls off his ball cap and changes it for his flying hat. It is another ball cap that simply says "Flying" on it. "Let me grab what I need, I'll meet you in the plane.

––––––––

WE LAND AND CATCH A CAB, HEADED STRAIGHT TO THE bar where Miles' red dot is flashing on the tracker's screen. Unless they removed the bullet on the plane, which I severely doubt - I know Miles has no pain tolerance - he should be right where it is flashing.

I signal the cab driver to stop two blocks down from the bar, where I throw a wad of cash on the front seat and grab our bags. Jake follows in step with me.

"So, what's the plan?" he whispers.

"We're not going to be able to go through the front door. We're going to go to the back alley and make our way to the roof."

Jake's footsteps fall silent behind me. I turn around to check on him and see he's standing still. "We're going to climb the building?"

"No, nothing that heroic. There's an old metal ladder leading up to the roof. Now come on." He falls in behind me again. We make it to the back of the building with no problems. One of his men was posted outside the front door, but there is no sign of anyone back here. I make sure my gun is snugly in place before beginning the climb. The first step creaks and I stop while both of us look around to make sure no one heard it. Once I know the coast is clear, I start climbing again. Jake waits at the bottom until I've made it all the way up the brick building. I throw my leg over the ledge and wave at him to start his climb.

Halfway up, someone comes around the corner. I motion for Jake to stop climbing and he hugs his body tight against the brick wall. I don't even think he's breathing. The guy looks around the area, but never looks up. I wave for Jake to continue his climb.

"That was some scary shit," he says, finally making it to the roof.

"It's only going to get worse. Are you sure you can handle it?"

"Now's a fine time to ask me that. Maybe you should have thought about that before you hijacked a plane and made me come with you."

Valid point, I never asked him. "Stay here. I'm going to go through the air vent. It drops down right into Miles' office. When it's done, I'll come back up using those stairs that are through that locked door." I point at them. "Your job is to find a way to get it unlocked before I come back up and to shoot anyone who comes through that door that isn't me. Can you handle that?"

He nods. I start to leave and he snags my arm. "I've never killed anyone before."

"Let's hope you don't have to. Come give me a boost to get into the vent system." Jake kneels down beneath it and laces his fingers together for me to step into. I step and he stands, giving me enough height to remove the outside frame and crawl inside.

I hear him whisper, "Be careful."

There is just enough room inside for me to crawl. Dust and mold are caked in a thick layer on the inside walls of the ductwork from years of abandonment. My movements kick up a cloud of dust, and I have to hold my breath to keep from coughing. I come to the first vent and look down. It's the office directly across from Miles. This will probably be a good place to enter, but first I want to see if Miles is in his office. Voices drift up to me as I crawl over the next vent. I lay down quietly and look through the slats. Miles is laying on his stomach on the desk and someone is removing the bullet from his shoulder.

"I should have killed the son of a bitch instead of blowing up his house. He has no idea the plans that have been set in motion for him." He's talking to one of his men who's leaning against the wall.

As far as I can tell, there are only three of them in the room. I wait and watch until the bullet is removed. The person that removed the bullet leaves the room and the guard follows, leaving Miles alone. Miles' stubby little arms are struggling their way into a button-down shirt. He moans when the shirt slides over his wound. "Damn it!" He sits down and lights up a cigarette. Time to make my move.

The crawl space is too tight for me to turn around. I slowly crawl backward to the previous vent and fish a multipurpose tool out of my pocket to unscrew the vent, careful not to make any noise. I slide it into the crawl space. Using my arms, I brace myself against the edges and lower myself down. My shoes make a dull thud as they hit the floor. I step behind the door in case someone comes in the room to see what it was.

Nothing. I don't hear anything. I peek out the door into the empty hallway, making sure the coast is clear before tiptoeing across the floor to Miles' office. He's got his feet propped up on his desk and I can see smoke billowing in front of him, completely unsuspecting. The element of surprise is on my side. I quietly step into the room. He looks up when he hears me shut the door.

He is already staring down the barrel of my gun. "How the hell did you get here?" His eyes are wide.

"Did you really think I would let you go?" My neck cracks as I cock my head to the side.

He raises his hands in the air. "I don't think you're as smart as you think you are." His eyes go to a drawer on his desk.

"Don't even think about." I walk closer.

He leans back in his chair. "You've left your family unprotected."

"I don't want to hear you mention my family ever again." I cock back the trigger on the gun.

"Let's talk about this." His hands are back in the air. "You don't really want to kill me."

"I want nothing more than to see the light fade from your beady little eyes. You've done nothing but ruin my life."

"You forget, I helped you get started in the business. I made you a lot of money to be able to take care of that brother of yours. You should be thanking me."

I huff out a laugh. "Thanking you? You kept me from Brooklyn for two years, then you tortured me with the knowledge of my son. You kill innocent people and you expect me to thank you?"

Something behind me slams me forward into the desk. I hold onto the gun with a death grip as my face is pressed into the desk. Miles reaches into a drawer and pulls something out before bolting for the door. I push back with all my strength and my assailant lands hard on the ground. I swing my arm around with the pistol, connecting the cold steel with his temple and knocking him out cold on the floor. I look up and catch a glimpse of Miles' backside as he hightails it out of the room.

I chase him up a flight of stairs while he screams wildly for his men to come help him. As his chubby feet land on the second step from the top, I dive forward and wrap my free hand around his ankle, causing him to stumble forward into the wall and slide to the ground. He lays there fumbling in his jacket pocket while I run up behind him. When he rolls over to face me, he has a grenade in his hand and his fingers around the pin. Reacting faster than he can process, I lunge forward again and grasp my hands around it. His fingers crunch beneath mine and he lets out an animal yelp before letting go of it. I get off the floor and stand above him. I shove my gun in the back of my belt, holding on tight to the grenade.

I glance down at the grenade in my hand and then at Miles. His eyes grow wide with understanding. "Don't do it," he shakes beneath me. "I'll never mess with your family again. You're a free man. All you have to do is walk away." He sits up.

"I'll be free when you are no longer breathing." I pull the pin and shove the grenade down the back of his shirt. "This is for blowing up Brooklyn's house." He screams as I take off up the next flight of stairs, hoping like hell Jake got the door unlocked - if not, I'm a dead man. The grenade detonates just as I reach the top step and the door flies open for me, the shockwave from the explosion throwing me like a ragdoll through to the other side.

Jake runs over and helps me get off the ground. "Run!" I yell. We take off toward the ladder.

"What the hell was that?" Jake is hauling ass down the stairs.

"It was Miles," I say with a grin, jumping down from the last few steps.

CHAPTER TWENTY-TWO

Brooklyn

I clutch my son to my chest, trying to calm him down while we wait for the fire department. I'm so relieved that we're all okay, but also annoyed because John had to run off to chase that asshole. Why couldn't he have just killed him here? None of this would've happened if he hadn't insisted on letting him get away.

I understand his reasoning, but I just wanted this all over. I want to move forward with my family, not spend more time dealing with the man who's ruined all our lives.

Red and white lights flash across the lawn, getting brighter as the fire truck pulls into the driveway. The guards usher us to the front of the property.

"Is this your house, ma'am?"

I nod. "Yes, it is," I answer the fireman.

"Do you know how the fire started?"

"No, I just heard a loud explosion. Everything happened so fast, I just wanted to make sure we all got out."

He nods. "Is everyone okay? Does anyone need medical attention?"

I look back at my dad, surrounded by his guards. "No, we're fine. Thank you."

He nods. "Okay, please stay back while we put out this fire." He runs off to join his the other firefighters.

I take the few steps to my dad and he puts his arm around me. "I have a car on the way to pick us up. How far is Jake's?"

"It's just down the road."

He rubs my back. "Everything will be okay, Brooky. It looks like most of the house is salvageable. Rebuild this section here and make a few repairs due to smoke damage and everything will be fine."

I nod. "I know, Dad."

The flames have been quenched. I look over at the sad, ruined home with a tear in my eye. I just hope John kills Miles this time. I want this done. I want my life back.

———

THE CAR COMES AND TAKES US TO JAKE'S HOUSE. I walk up the front steps and unlock the door with the key Jake left for us. It's still dark, so I turn on a few lights and show my dad to the guest bedroom.

I give John a bath and rock him to sleep. He's so tired from the stress of everything that all it takes to send him off into a deep, peaceful sleep is a cup of warm milk. I place him in the bed and head to the bathroom to shower.

Stepping out, I feel like everything has washed away. I no longer smell the smoke on me or feel the heat of the flames licking my skin. I pull on a pair of Jake's sweatpants and find a T-shirt that I can wear before climbing into bed with J-Man.

A piece of me feels like it is missing. John is off chasing after Miles who will lead him God knows where. What if he never comes back? What if Miles gets the upper hand again? And this time, it won't just be John, but Jake too. I don't know what I would've done without Jake all these years. He really is like a brother to me now. I just pray that I don't lose either one of them.

———

JOHN WAKES ME UP IN THE MORNING, SITTING UP AND playing with my hair. Bright light bleeds between the slats in the blinds, lighting the room.

I smile when I see his eyes meet mine. "Good morning, baby. Are you ready for some breakfast?"

He squeals and claps his hands, trying to stand up on the bed, but loses his balance and falls over onto his back.

I laugh before helping him off the bed and down to the kitchen. "Good morning, Dad," I say as I hand him Little Man.

"Good morning. Any word from the two superheroes?"

I pour a mug of coffee, chuckling to myself. "Not yet." I set the pot down. "Should I be worried?" I look over at him.

"Nah, not yet. I'm sure they'll call soon."

Jake's fridge is empty, other than a half-full gallon of milk. I hand John a cup of it and rummage through the cabinets and pantry to find something for breakfast. Nothing there either. I check the freezer and, lucky me, find some frozen waffles and sausage patties.

I shrug and pull out the items. "I hope you like frozen waffles."

Dad waves me off, too busy playing with his grandson to care what we eat.

I pop the waffles into the toaster and the sausage patties in the microwave. While they cook, I walk over and take John from my dad. "I'm going to get him dressed before we eat." I walk him into the bedroom that Jake keeps stocked with John's things for when he babysits.

J-Man crawls around on the floor while I dig a shirt and shorts out of the small dresser.

As I'm pulling the shirt over his head, I hear the crack of gunfire, accompanied by shattering glass. Someone yells, "Get down!"

I grab John and walk along the edge of the wall to peek into the living room. My dad is lying on the floor with a guard hovering over him. There is blood everywhere.

"Dad!" I scream and move to step out.

The guard turns toward me. "Don't move. I don't want you hurt. Stay where you are until the perimeter is cleared.

I nod and choke back a sob, feeling trapped. I want to run to my dad and check on him, but I can't. All I can do is watch while the guard applies pressure to the wound on his chest and calls 911.

"Is he going to be okay?" I ask, tears filling my eyes.

"I don't know." I can hear the worry in his voice and it only worries me more.

The house phone rings and I slip into a bedroom to answer it. "Hello?"

"It's me. I got him. It's over," John says on the other side of the line.

The tears finally overfill my eyes as I shake my head. "It's not over yet. My dad's just been shot."

"What? Where are you?"

"We came to Jake's last night. They shot him through the window. I don't know if he's going to be okay. The ambulance is on its way."

"Fuck! This was his plan the whole time. He just drew me away so he could take out his target. If that son of a bitch wasn't dead already, I'd kill him again."

I sniffle as I fall onto the bed. "Get home soon, John."

"We're on our way," he promises.

"Oh, and John?"

"Yeah?"

"I love you," I say, a little breathless.

"I love you, too. We'll be right there."

I hang up the phone and rush back to the hallway to see what is going on. The guard sees me and says,

"The perimeter is secure, ma'am. The shooter has been taken out."

I rush to my father's side and fall to my knees while holding on to little man. "Is he breathing?"

The guard nods. "Yes, but it's shallow."

I look at my dad's closed eyes. He looks so peaceful, like he's just sleeping. The color is slowly draining from his face.

It feels like forever but the EMT's finally rush in and strap him on the gurney, rushing him out of the house and into the ambulance.

Little man and I climb into my dad's rental car with two of the guards and we follow behind it.

————

I CALL GRACE, THE NANNY, AND SHE MEETS US AT THE hospital. When she arrives, I hand John to her and ask her to keep him occupied while I track down a nurse.

They've had my dad back in surgery for what seems like forever now, and so far, no updates.

I'm a nervous wreck without John here and with my dad in surgery. Nervous energy has me bouncing off the walls. I can't just sit and wait, I have to do something.

I head over to the nurses' station and wait for one of them to come back.

"Can I help you?"

"Yes, do you have any information on my father? He's been in surgery for two hours now."

She's seen me many times so she knows who I am and who my father is. "Not yet, miss. I promise as soon as I get word, I will come find you. Now, please, just try to relax."

I take a deep breath to keep myself from yelling at the poor nurse, who's doing everything she can to keep me calm. I know none of this is her fault, but I'm so scared and anxious that I can't sit still.

I force a smile and nod at her before turning around.

Back in the waiting room, I sit down in the floor with John and Grace. We take turns rolling a small ball back and forth. John laughs and squeals when he catches it and it helps to ease away my fears. I keep my mind busy by playing with him and before I know it, the nurse is walking out.

When she comes to a stop, I stand. It feels like the world has stopped spinning as I hold my breath.

"Your dad is out of surgery. Everything is fine."

I let out a long breath and my shoulders fall. "Can I see him?"

"Soon. He lost a lot of blood, and he's still in recovery. But when he wakes and we have him settled in a room, you'll be the first to go back," she promises.

"Thank you," I tell her, shaking her hand.

I sit down in a chair and finally allow myself to breathe. My dad is going to be okay, John and Jake are on their way back, and Miles is out of our lives for good. A huge weight has been lifted from my shoulders.

————

THE SUN IS JUST FALLING BELOW THE HORIZON through the window of my dad's room when the door opens and John and Jake rush in. John rushes over and pulls me into his arms.

"I'm so glad you're okay."

He kisses my lips quickly. "He is going to be okay?" He nods toward my dad, who is asleep in his hospital bed.

I nod. "He lost a lot of blood and they are keeping him heavily medicated for now, but yes, he'll be fine."

"Thank God. I'm so sorry for leaving you. I wasn't thinking clearly. I just had to get Miles out of our lives."

I place my hand on his cheek, directing his eyes to me instead of my father. "It's okay. We're all fine and Miles is gone for good. What more could I ask for?" My lips find his again, but this time, they linger a little longer. I want to feel him, taste him, and remind myself that this is all over and that we can finally move on. No more being hunted or chased. Just us, living happily ever after.

"Where's L.J.?" John asks.

"L.J.?" I ask, wrinkling my brow.

John shrugs. "I've been trying to think up a new nickname for him. J-Man won't work forever, and Little John sounds too much like Robin Hood. I thought L.J. would be good."

I smile and nod. "I like it." I pull myself against his chest and let his arms wrap around me before answering his question.

"The nanny took him down to the cafeteria to eat some dinner."

John and Jake sit down in the chairs on either side of my dad's bed and I curl up with my head in John's lap. He wraps his arms around me and kisses the top of my head.

Jake looks bored already and pulls out his phone. I see his brows furrow together while his eyes focus on something.

"What?" I ask him, nerves starting to rev back up.

He looks up at us. "I just noticed that I got an email from your security company."

I sit up. "What's it say?"

"It says that a silent alarm was tripped two days before we got home. They sent someone out to check on it but didn't find anything."

"That's strange," I say, leaning back into John's chest.

"That must have been when they set up the explosives," John says from behind me.

I turn to face him. "But how? Didn't you two watch the video leading up to the day we arrived?"

"They must have tampered with it," John says.

"Can they do that?" I ask.

He shrugs. "It wouldn't be the first time. I wonder what kind of shape the video feed is in back at the house."

Jake shows us his cell phone. "It all gets backed up to the cloud. I can access it from right here."

John and I stand behind Jake, peering over his shoulder. We watch as he pulls up the security feed from the day the alarm was tripped. He plays the video in fast forward, but we don't catch anything.

"Wait, go back," John says.

Jake rewinds back a few minutes and hits *play* again.

The video is from the camera that is pointing at the back door. I don't see anything out of the ordinary.

"What? I don't see anything."

"Look right here in this clip." He points at a leaf falling from the tree.

"So? It's a leaf, those fall all the time."

He shakes his head. "In this frame, the leaf is falling, but in the very next frame, the leaf is lying on the ground. So somehow it went from mid-air to being on the ground. There is a whole section of video that was removed."

Jake plays it again, and we all watch a little closer. He's right. It isn't something that most people would pick up or notice since the main focus is on the backdoor.

I shrug. "Well, it doesn't matter now. Too bad we didn't notice this a few days ago. We might still have a house left." I walk over to the window and look out.

John stands upright and walks over to me, wrapping his arms around me. "We will rebuild. Everything will be fine. All that matters is we're all safe and we don't have to worry about Miles ever again. We're free." His dark eyes meet mine.

"We're free," I repeat before moving in for another kiss.

CHAPTER TWENTY-THREE

John

"It looks better than ever." I kiss the back of Brooklyn's head as we stand back looking at the house. So much has changed in the last nine months. Freedom, for the first time in years. Happiness like I've never experienced. A legit job. I opened a shooting range and teach classes for concealed weapons permits. It's the perfect job for me. I even exposed all of Miles' clients to get rid of my guilt. Even the nightmares have all but stopped. I have peace for the first time in my life.

"I'm glad we built the additions. Dad is going to love living on the property now that his term is over. He loves spending time with L.J."

"He will love spending time with this one too." I splay my hand out on her pregnant belly. "I can't wait for her to make her arrival in a few more weeks."

She turns in my arms. "She could make her arrival today and I'd be okay with that. I'm tired of being pregnant."

"I don't know... I think you're rather sexy pregnant. I think I'll keep you barefoot and pregnant," I tease with her.

"Oh no you won't. Snip snip for you, mister." She forms scissors with her fingers and makes a cutting motion.

I step away from her, covering my boys. "That's a little harsh, don't you think?"

"Harsh?" she laughs. "Try delivering a bowling ball out of your vagina."

I cringe at the thought. "How about we find a compromise?" I pull her back into me.

"The only compromise you get is if you don't get fixed, you won't be getting that thing near me."

"You are one tough woman." I kiss her pouting lips. "You can't live without sex any more than I can."

"Try me."

"It's bad enough that I've actually had to endure hearing you have sex, but do you have to talk about it too?" Jake walks by carrying a bottle of champagne.

I take Brook's hand and she waddles beside me. "You're just jealous. When's the last time you got laid?"

"Actually, I met someone and I have high hopes for the weekend." He wears a cheesy smile on his face.

"Really? Are we going to get to meet her?" I ask, following him inside the house.

"Not a chance in hell am I letting her meet you." He walks straight into the newly designed kitchen and pops the bottle open.

"Why? Are you afraid your better-looking twin may charm her away from you?" Brooklyn's hand lands upside my head. "Ow!"

"You're an idiot!" Jake chuckles.

Matthew walks in holding L.J. in one arm and a file in another. He throws it on the counter in front of me and grabs one of the champagne glasses. "It's finally completed. My last act as President of the United States." He tips his glass and drinks it down.

"Is that his pardon?" Brooklyn is bouncing up and down clapping her hands. L.J. mimics her.

"Yes, it is. All your sins have been forgiven," Matthew says.

"I can't believe it's finally over." In my excitement I pick up Brooklyn and twirl her around. When I put her back on her feet, I take L.J. from Matthew and kiss his cheek. I'm finally going to be a man my family can be proud of.

"Uh... John," Brooklyn says. "I think my water just broke." She's standing stock-still looking down at the puddle on the ground.

"Everything is going to be okay. Jake, go get the car." He takes off running. "Matthew, there is a bag at the foot of our bed. Go get it. I'll take Brooklyn and John to the car."

———

WE ARRIVE AT THE HOSPITAL IN THE MIDDLE OF A contraction. "Wait, just give me a minute," Brooklyn yells from the back seat. Her contractions are coming hard and fast and I'm starting to panic.

"I'll go get a wheelchair." I run inside the emergency room doors and grab the first one I see. Matthew has Brooklyn on his arm when I make it back to the car. Jake is holding L.J.

"Here. Sit." I place it behind Brooklyn. She gingerly sits down. I take off in a run.

"Whoa, slow down, you're making me nauseous." Brooklyn places her hand on her mouth.

"Sorry, just a little excited." I slow my pace.

Matthew holds the door open and I take her directly to the triage desk. "Excuse me, but my wife is in labor."

"Fill out the paperwork and we'll be right with you," the nurse says.

"But, she's having contractions."

"It's okay, John. Just fill them out." Brooklyn pats my hand.

I quickly write in a few pertinent things and hand the clipboard back to her. She stands and says, "Right this way."

Our group steps into the elevator and gets off on the third floor. The nurse talks to the other nurse at the desk. She smiles sweetly and then tells us we will need to wait out here until the doctor checks her out. She points us in the direction of the waiting room.

Nobody else is in here, so we take over the room. "I'm not very good at this part," I say, starting to pace the room.

"What part is that?" Matthew asks.

"Waiting."

He lets out a laugh. "Don't we all know it. You would only wait a week after you got back to marry my daughter."

He's right. I didn't want to waste any more time, but neither did Brooklyn. We were all crammed into Matthew's hospital room. She wore a beautifully-fitted white gown with sequins all down it. Her red locks of hair were draped off one shoulder. Her shiny white heels put her right at my height. She was absolutely stunning. At that very moment, I was the luckiest man alive. I had her on one arm and my son on the other. We truly became a family that day. Here we are now, almost nine months later to the date, adding to our family.

I was out back helping build Matthew's bungalow, when Brooklyn came outside holding a cake and bag of paper plates. I remember thinking it was kind of odd, but she loved to cook so I played along when she asked if I wanted a slice. She laid the cake on a makeshift table and sliced into it. She handed me the plate and I stared at the cake. The frosting was white, but the inside was two different colors. Pink and blue. It took me minute to figure out what she was trying to tell me. I threw the plate on the ground and picked her up off the ground, kissing her like I never had before.

"Mr. Remington, you can come back and see your wife now." A nurse pops her head into the room.

I turn to look at L.J. who is in the process of ripping up some magazines. "I got him, you go," Jake says.

"Thanks." I follow the nurse to Brooklyn's room. She's hooked to all kinds of monitors. Fear sets in.

"Are you okay?" I point to the machines and she giggles.

"This is all perfectly normal." I sit on the bed next to her. "I'm already eight centimeters, so it won't be long now.

I watch the monitor as the lines start going up. "What does that mean?" I figure it out when I start to lose all the feeling in my hand from the death grip Brooklyn has on it. "Oh, okay, breathe. We practiced this in Lamaze class." She nods her head. Her hand starts to loosen and I know her contraction is easing up.

An hour later, the room is filled with nurses and a doctor. Brooklyn has been pushing for almost thirty minutes. "I see the baby's head," the doctor announces.

I move around where I can see and Brook yanks me back. "I don't want you passing out like your brother." I stay where she wants me until our daughter makes her arrival and I get to cut the cord. I don't know what all the fuss was with Jake, she's beautiful.

The nurse wraps a blanket around her and hands her to me. "She's got a set of lungs," I say, laying her on Brooklyn. "She looks like you." I kiss Brooklyn on the head and sit down beside her.

A few minutes later the doctor leaves and the nurse has our daughter all cleaned up. She's settled down, but she is wide-eyed. "She has your eyes," Brooklyn coos.

Her tiny hand has a tight grip on my little finger. "I can see hints of red in her hair already."

Jake and Matthew barge into the room, spoiling our moment. Jake hands me John and he and Matthew fight over who is going to hold the baby. Brooklyn and I laugh at them.

"So, does my new granddaughter have a name?" he asks, leaning over Jake's shoulder looking at her.

"We named her Jacquelyn." Brooklyn says. I watch for it to register on Matthew's face.

"After your mother." His eyes start to water. "She would be so proud of you."

I lean over and kiss Brooklyn on the lips. "I'm proud of you, too. You're such a remarkable woman. All of our lives are better because of you, including the millions of people who were cured of cancer. I don't deserve you, but I plan on being the man you need for the rest of our lives together. John and Jacquelyn will never know what my life was like before. All they will ever know is how much they are loved, and how much I love and cherish their mother."

"I love you too, John," she whispers as she kisses me softly.

***

WILL JAKE REMINGTON EMERGE A NEW HERO, OR WILL he become the sacrificial lamb for his brother's sins? Hold Onto Me

Falling Hard is FREE when you join Newsletter.

Thank you for reading *Stay With Me.* Your honest review will help future readers decide if they want to take a chance on a new-to-them author.

ABOUT AUTHOR KELLY MOORE

"This author has the magical ability to take an already strong and interesting plot and add so many unexpected twists and turns that it turns her books into a complete addiction for the reader." Dandelion Inspired Blog

Join Newsletter to stay up-to-date.

Armed with books in the crook of my elbow, I can go anywhere. That's my philosophy! Better yet, I'll write the books that will take me on an adventure.

My heroes are a bit broken but will make you swoon. My heroines are their own kick-ass characters armed with humor and a plethora of sarcasm.

If I'm not tucked away in my writing den, with coffee firmly gripped in hand, you can find me with a book propped on my pillow, a pit bull lying across my legs, a Lab on the floor next to me, and two kittens running amuck.

My current adventure has me living in Idaho with my own gray-bearded hero, who's put up with my shenanigans for over thirty years, and he doesn't mind all my book boyfriends.

If you love romance, suspense, military men, lots of action and adventure infused with emotion, tear-worthy moments, and laugh-out-loud humor, dive into my books and let the world fall away at your feet.

SERIES

Whiskey River West

Whiskey River Road

Elite Six Series

The Revenge You Seek

The Vigilante Hitman

August Series

Epic Love Stories

For more follow me on Amazon for a detailed list of books.

Or, on my website at kellymooreauthor.com

Made in the USA
Columbia, SC
03 May 2025

57483140R00180